A TEASPOON OF MISTLETOE

BARBARA MCMAHON

A Teaspoon of Mistletoe
Copyright © 2018 Barbara McMahon
All Rights Reserved

This is a work of fiction. Names, characters, places and incidents are products of the author's imagination and are used fictitiously. Any resemblance to actual events, locales, organizations or persons living or dead is entirely coincidental.

1

Annie Tolliver reached up to fasten the large wreath onto the light pole's small cross beam. Only twenty more to go and she'd have all the street lights in the park adorn with Christmas wreaths. It was bitterly cold, so as she drove her pickup truck to the next pole, she held first one hand and then the other to the vent in the truck pumping out warm air. She couldn't wear gloves; the fasteners were hard enough to connect with her bare fingers. Adding bulky gloves and she'd never finish.

As she rounded the slight curve in the wide pathway, she noticed a man sitting on one of the benches facing the park and playground area. There wasn't another soul around. No wonder, it was barely daylight.

Wasn't he freezing, she wondered. She was. If she didn't have to get all the wreaths up today she'd have waited until later in the morning when the temperature might rise above freezing. But she had other things to do today and so had started early.

She pulled close to the next pole, got out, climbed into the back of her truck and picked up another wreath. She loved the smell of the evergreen, though sticky residue was its legacy. Still, she was happy to have garnered the contract from the city to decorate the parks. This was the last one.

In January, she'd retrace her route to remove all the wreaths.

She liked the way the wreaths added a festive seasonal touch to the walkways. Christmas was her favorite holiday. Peace and joy and good will to all seemed to permeate the entire town at this time of year.

Two more poles and she'd reach the man sitting on the bench. He hadn't appeared to move since she first saw him. He was all right, wasn't he? She moved to the next pole. Getting the wreaths up early made sense because so many people used the walk way during the day, she wouldn't feel right with her truck on the path. But she needed its bed to reach the cross beams.

When Annie pulled even with the bench, she gave him a worried glance.

Was he dead?

She didn't know anyone in their right mind who would take a nap on a park bench in below freezing weather.

Oh no, what if he'd been here all night?

Suddenly she knew she had to make sure he was all right. She scrambled from the truck and approached.

"Hello?" she said.

There was no response. His head dropped forward so she couldn't see him clearly.

She'd had CPR training a while ago–thinking to be prepared, but right now her mind went blank. Was it thirty compressions and then a breath, or fifteen and then a breath and then more compression? And shouldn't he be lying down to get CPR?

Gently she touched his neck. She couldn't feel a pulse. His skin was as cold as ice.

What if he was dead? What if he wasn't?

She tried to unzip the jacket. She'd have to try CPR. Glancing around, she didn't see another soul in the park. Dare she pull him off the bench to get him to lie flat on the ground?

He came awake with a start.

"What the heck?" he said, as his hand gripped her wrist. "What do you think you're doing?" he asked, standing and towering over Annie, his hand tightening.

"Good, you're alive," she said in relief.

"Of course I'm alive."

"Well, I wondered. I mean it's sort of cold out and I'm not sure sleeping in the park in this weather such a good idea. I thought you might be dead and I was trying to remember my CPR training."

He shook his head as if to clear it and then released her wrist.

"If I were already dead, no CPR in the world would have revived me," he said, zipping his jacket up again.

Annie nodded. That made sense. "So I was hoping you weren't already dead," she said, feeling flustered looking into his dark eyes. His expression reflected exasperation and she took a step back.

"Do you always rush to rescue someone whether they need it or not?" he demanded.

She thought about it for a minute and then shrugged.

"I guess I've never found anyone in need of rescue before, but yes, I'd try to help."

"I don't need rescuing," he said.

"Well, excuse me for thinking you did."

He could have been a little grateful for her efforts.

He stood several inches taller than her own five feet five inches. His skin was pale and he looked awfully thin. What was he doing sitting in the below freezing weather? Sleeping in it actually.

She hadn't seen him before; she would have remembered that face. Not that she knew everyone in Lamberton, but still—this was a man she wouldn't have forgotten.

He looked around and gazed a moment on her truck.

"Don't let me keep you," he said.

She narrowed her eyes: "Are you going back to sleep? Maybe you should post a sign—don't try to save me, I like sleeping in below freezing weather."

"What I do is no concern of yours."

"Well, you have that right."

She spun around and stomped back to her truck. She was only trying to help. What if he had been near death? She was the only one any where around who could have saved him. Then he'd be singing a different tune.

"Thanks for stopping" he called as she reached her truck, "not everyone would. I could have ended up with frostbite," he said as his hands covered his ears. He didn't wear gloves or a hat.

Which seemed foolish to Annie. It was supposed to hover around freezing all week. And snow by the weekend. Sitting on a park bench in the dead of winter wasn't her idea of a good time.

"Maybe you should head to Margie's Coffee Stand, just around that bend. She'll be opened by now. Lots of folks stop by on their way to work. Get a hot coffee or hot cocoa or something to warm up with," Annie suggested, a bit appeased by his belated thanks.

He nodded, looking in the direction she pointed.

She gave a small wave and got back to her truck. She still had the rest of those wreaths to put up.

Annie watched as he walked away. Maybe she should have invited him into the warm cab, but she didn't know him and wasn't that foolish.

Moving on to the next pole she wondered what he was doing sitting out so early in such cold weather. Was he new in town or just visiting someone for the holidays?

The jacket he wore looked warm enough, but who walked around Montana in the dead of winter with no hat and gloves?

Her curiosity peaked. Who was he? And why was he sleeping on a park bench? He didn't look homeless. His clothes were clean and fairly new.

He was apparently in no hurry to get to a job. It was now after eight, most people were heading to or already at work. So maybe he was a visitor.

By the time Annie arrived at Margie's for her own warm up, her mysterious acquaintance stood at the kiosk chatting with the owner. Margie ran the small beverage kiosk summer and winter, varying the offerings depending upon the weather. Hot chocolate and hot coffee were her winter specialties. She offered to top off any drink with either whipped cream or marshmallows.

Annie always chose the marshmallows.

"Hi, Margie," she said after she parked the truck and approached the open serving window.

"Hi, Annie. The park looks really good. I wandered through yesterday afternoon."

"Thanks, I put the last of the wreaths up this morning. Next up is the Santa's Workshop."

"So, what can I get you?"

"I'll have the hot chocolate with marshmallows."

Annie glanced at the man standing beside her. "I see you found it."

He nodded, taking a sip of a hot beverage he held in his hand.

"We never did introduce ourselves; I'm Annie Tolliver, landscaper and Christmas decorator."

"Nick Keller, visitor for a few weeks." He offered his hand.

It was like ice.

Annie had a sudden urge to wrap both her hands around his to warm it up.

There were benches along the walk way, but as cold as it was she didn't want to sit outside once she had her hot chocolate. But it felt rude to walk away.

With Margie only a few feet away, she felt safe enough to invite him into the truck cab where they'd be warm.

"Do you want to sit in my truck while we drink?" she asked.

Nick hesitated a moment as if weighing a mighty decision, then nodded.

Once inside, she started the engine again to get the heater working.

"Did you decorate the entire park?" Nick asked when they were seated.

"Yes. Well, my team and I did. We put up the Christmas lights last week. The tree near the bandstand was decorated on Thanksgiving so the town could kick off the annual lighting of the tree and Main Street Festival the Friday after Thanksgiving. Were you here then?"

"No, I arrived a few days ago."

Annie was dying to find out more, but didn't want to appear too nosy. Could a few questions be considered interested instead of nosy?

"So you're not from here. Where are you from?" she asked.

"Originally, Oregon. Most recently sub Sahara Africa."

"Africa, wow. What did you do there?" She'd never met anyone who had been to Africa.

"I'm with Doctors Without Borders. Most recently we went in to help with an epidemic."

She'd heard of Doctors Without Borders—they were responders to crises, whether an epidemic or natural disaster, and were totally neutral, so were able to go about everywhere to offer assistance.

"Yet Montana is a far piece from Africa," she murmured.

"I have a cousin who lives here—Roger Keller. He's at a conference in Chicago right now. Then he's taking off for the Bahamas for Christmas. He offered me his place for as long as I want. Do you know him?"

"I know of him--he's one of the town's leading young lawyers. If you have a perfectly comfortable place to stay, can I ask why you were sitting out in the freezing cold?" she asked, still intrigued.

He smiled.

Oh oh, that smile flustered her more than anything. His entire face seemed to soften a bit. Still strong and masculine, but with almost a hint of a mischievous boy.

"It might sound dumb, but after the heat and humidity of Africa, I can't get enough of the cold crisp air here. I'm walking as much as I can each day to enjoy the weather. I was out before dawn and sat for a moment to watch the sunrise. Guess I was more tired than I thought. Time change and all."

Annie nodded, taking a sip of her hot chocolate. "So you're a doctor?"

He nodded, his hands wrapped around the hot beverage.

"Tell me about decorating the park," he said. "Do you do it every Christmas?"

Annie explained how she bid for the job each year and so far in the five years she'd had her landscape business, she'd won the contract each year. She and her employees strung lights and placed large ornaments on the town's Christmas tree. Then she'd threaded tiny white lights through the trees and shrubbery around the walkways in the park. They'd build the Santa's Workshop near the gazebo by the Christmas tree and today she was putting up the wreaths.

"So you're finished, now," he said.

"Almost—we still need to decorate Santa's Workshop so we can open up on Saturday. It's open each weekend until Christmas. Then in January, we take everything down and pack away for next year. The wreaths of course go to recycle. I make them without wires so they can be disposed of easily."

"It sounds like a lot of work."

"It is, but there's not a lot of landscape work needed this time of year. So I bid for this job to keep income coming in. At my nursery I have poinsettias for sale, and some smaller wreaths and of course Christmas trees and ornaments for sale. Do you need a tree?"

He shook his head. "I'm not much for decorating."

"Everyone should decorate their home for Christmas," she said.

"Ah, but this isn't my home. I'm just visiting."

"Let me guess, your cousin left before he decorated."

Nick nodded.

"But wouldn't you like to have a small tree? Something to celebrate the season?"

"I suppose you have just the tree for me," he said, looking directly at her.

"Well, I do, but you don't have to buy one from me. There're other tree lots in town."

"Tell me about the town. This is only the second time I've been here. I visited Roger a few years back, during one week in the summer and we spent most of the time hiking the mountains."

"Lamberton was once a gold mining town, as your cousin might have mentioned. There're still some mines around that give tours in the summer. Now, it's just a small mountain town that has no major industry except ranching, no major chain stores who think we're too small, and no claim to fame. But I've lived here my entire life and love it. It's an active community with things going on all the time. If you lived in a small town in Oregon growing up, you probably had the same kind of things going on."

"Portland isn't such a small town. What small town things is Lamberton doing for Christmas?" he asked.

"We had the Main Street Festival the Friday after Thanksgiving. It's where all the shops are open late and serve Christmas cookies and hot cider to all who enter. That followed the tree lighting ceremony in the park. Then we have Santa's Workshop."

He nodded. "I've seen it when cutting through the park."

"Then we have a gift drop-off at the community center where people can donate gifts for kids who might not have a special Christmas otherwise. Volunteers wrap and deliver the gifts. I volunteer for that. I can deliver a lot using my truck."

Annie glanced at Nick who was gazing at her

steadily as she spoke. She swallowed. Her truck suited her all the time, except this morning it seemed smaller somehow.

Or maybe Nick just took up more space.

"There's the Christmas play next weekend—with folks of all ages participating. It's funny and fun. You should go," she said.

He nodded, but made no response. His hands were wrapped around the cup, obviously seeking the warmth.

The heater continued to pump hot air into the cab of the truck. With the hot chocolate, heater and Nick's proximity, Annie was starting to get warm.

"On Christmas Eve, there's a huge potluck at the community center with midnight services at several churches afterward. It seems the whole town gets together at one of the other events."

"Sounds idealistic. Not many places still do so much," he said.

"Maybe it's because we're a rather small community. We know each other and keep it local. Though we do get visitors who come each year because of the activities. I think it's fun for them to pretend to live in a town with traditions we have," Annie said. "That's part of the holiday magic, don't you think—following family traditions."

Nick took a long drink of his beverage,

finishing it. "Maybe if you have a family. But some of us don't."

He opened the door and began to get out of the warm truck.

"Do you need a lift home?" she asked, suddenly reluctant to have him leave.

"No need. Good bye."

He closed the door a walked away after tossing his empty cup in the trash next to Margie's kiosk.

"I hope I see you again," Annie said slowly as she watched him in the rearview mirror head back the way he'd come.

Nick felt exhausted by the time he reached the condo. He removed his jacket and tossed it on the back of the sofa on his way to the recliner. Sinking back, he closed his eyes. He was such a mess. He'd been up for four hours, already had a short nap in the park and now wanted nothing more than to sleep a week.

He knew he'd waken long before he was rested, but giving into temptation, he closed eyes.

But instead of dropping off to sleep immediately, he thought about Annie Tolliver. She reminded him of the classic girl next door. She had brown hair that peeped out from beneath her knitted stocking cap and a sprinkle of freckles across her nose. Her eyes were a warm and friendly brown. He wished he could have talked to her for longer. But his energy level wasn't even close to being back to normal and even the hot chocolate couldn't give him enough energy.

One day, he'd be back in fighting form. It was taking longer than he liked. As a doctor he knew the body healed in its own time. He grew impatient with the duration. He needed to get back.

Or did he?

He'd wanted to join Doctors Without Borders since he'd been a kid and first heard about them. His medical education was broad and he hadn't specialized in any one field, but wanted a wide background. He'd learned so much about various diseases in his work over the last few years and gained experience in tropical diseases far beyond what he would have had he opened a family practice in the states.

He'd dealt with more traumas than expected during natural disasters. Every bit of knowledge helped with future patients.

But it got tiring being in foreign countries all the time.

He frowned. That was one of the things that had appealed when he was studying in med school—variety and travel.

It was a nomadic life and he wasn't sure how much longer he'd enjoy that. He only had time to learn enough of a language to work with patients, then they'd move on. His colleagues came from a variety of countries. All spoke some English and he was at least conversant in French. He liked working with them.

If he was being honest with himself, he'd have to confess that sometimes late, at night, he felt all alone in a foreign place.

His mother had died while he'd been in medical school. His father had remarried a few years later to a widow with several young children. He was in his element participating in all the activities of children growing up.

Nick kept in touch via Skype, but they hadn't seen each other in a couple of years.

He himself was thirty-eight years old. He'd had the opportunities in his life he'd once wanted. Now, what?

Was it a result of this illness that he was even questioning things?

Maybe it was time to settle some place and change the direction of his life. Maybe that dream had played out and a new one was ready to take hold.

This town, the activities Annie had related, had him thinking even more about putting down roots. It sounded very appealing to become a part of a community that he'd never have to leave for the next outbreak of a deadly disease. To establish a practice and get to know his patients when well and sick.

Right now, however, it was merely something to think about, not time to make any hasty decisions. Some of these thoughts could be the reactions to being so sick.

He'd continue to take one day at a time. Focus on building back his strength and energy, and let the future stay uncertain until he was ready to make a choice.

2

After lunch, Nick bundled up again and went to walk around his neighborhood. There were few people around due, he thought, to the frigid temperature. To him it was a welcomed relief after the heat of Africa. Relishing every moment, he pushed himself to go farther to see as much of the town as he could.

It was charming in an old west kind of way. When he walked down Main Street, he noticed the wooden false fronts on some of the buildings. The signs in front of two indicated they were more than a hundred years old.

He almost expected to see cowboys ride up on horseback, tie the horses to a hitching rail and mosey on into a saloon. Except, he didn't notice any saloons on the street.

At the far end was the large community building where the town events were held—including that potluck Annie had spoken about. He wandered down the street, gazing at the Christmas decorations adorning each shop. Some were simple and small, others elaborate and expansive. It was obvious that Christmas was a special holiday in Lamberton. And vastly different from the holidays he'd spent abroad.

Europe also dazzled with decorations, but more years than not, he'd been in some poor African village working around the clock and completely missing the holiday.

When he reached the community center, he noticed the glass encased bulletin board by the door full of announcements of forthcoming events.

He studied the calendar. If he was serious about returning for good to the US, he might as well attend these to see what it was like. Lamberton was a nice town, from what his cousin said. He could consider staying here if there was any need for another doctor.

And if he did, he'd likely see Annie Tolliver often.

On the other hand, his work over the last few years had been rewarding–taking medical knowledge into areas totally lacking in even basic care.

Yet, as being so sick showed him, he was not infallible. Doctors got sick. Died. Maybe it was time to reevaluate, make new goals or plans.

The next morning Nick was again up early. Too bad all the decorations in the park had been put in place or he might run into Annie again. Still, feeling refreshed after a long night's sleep he decided to head for the coffee house at one end of Main Street and treat himself to a sugary treat and designer coffee–both an amazing luxury after the remote locations he normally inhabited.

The shop was crowded when he entered and hot. Loosening his jacket, he stood in line. He hadn't expected the place to be to be so busy. Checking the time he realized it was shortly before eight and most of those in line probably were getting their beverages to go. He looked to the left where the tables were. Several were empty. Annie sat at one with a large cup in front of her. She was reading something on a tablet and seemed totally oblivious to the commotion around her.

When Nick placed his order, he glanced around again to look at Annie.

She was still focused on the tablet. Would she welcome an interruption or be annoyed?

No time like the present to find out.

Once coffee and cinnamon roll were in hand, he walked over to her table.

"Mind if I join you?" he asked.

She looked up in surprise, then a wide smile lit her face. "Hi. Yes, do join me. Came in out of the cold today?"

He placed his breakfast on the small table and shrugged out of his jacket. After the frigid air outside, this place seemed stifling. "I plan to head to the park after I eat."

She looked at the huge sweet roll and grinned at him.

"I'd think a doctor would eat differently," she said with a teasing note in her voice.

"I'm indulging myself. No cinnamon rolls where I've been the last few years."

He took a big bite of the treat and savored every taste sensation.

"I've been walking around Lamberton," he said a moment later. "It's a nice town."

"I think so. It's not as big a tourist draw as some people would like, but we do get visitors for special events–like the Christmas season, Gold Rush days in the spring and for the Independence Day celebrations," she responded. "Some people like the small town feel of the place, and the old-fashioned celebrations."

"I can understand the appeal," he said, taking another bite. He should have come here before now. The cinnamon roll was beyond delicious.

"Tell me about where you practiced medicine; I know it has to be vastly different from here."

He remembered some of the places he'd been and nodded. None were like this western town.

"Parts of Africa are amazingly beautiful like Victoria Falls and Mount Kilimanjaro. Other places are desert, devoid of much but barren land. Hauntingly beautiful none the less in its own way. But mostly I was involved with disasters and epidemics and focused on the people who needed aid."

"How long before you return?" Annie asked.

He shrugged. Everyone thought he'd return. It was only in the last couple of days that doubt rose.

"After the holidays."

"Great, you came at the best time. You will check out all the activities, right?"

He nodded. She was getting to him.

"So do you recommend everyone begin their day with an overdose of sugar?" she teased again.

Nick glanced at the almost gone cinnamon roll. She wasn't going to guilt him into regretting one single bite.

"No, only those from Africa who haven't had a cinnamon roll in years," he replied giving her a lopsided grin.

She grinned back. Taking a final sip of her beverage, she put the cup down and gathered her tablet.

"I have to get to work," she said, putting her tablet in her large purse and reaching for the empty coffee cup.

"Need any help?" he asked.

Where had that come from? He'd just met the woman. She ran her own nursery—obviously with employees to help in the workload.

She looked surprised. "Not really. If you want to ride along, I'm delivering poinsettia to offices which have ordered them for the season. Then I have some plants to check on at the local nursing home."

Annie was surprised at his offer, but understood he was probably tired of his being alone and knowing no one in town. And truth be told, she wouldn't mind his company. Her curiosity seemed to rise each time she saw him.

He popped the last bite of the roll in his mouth, wiped his lips with the napkin and balled it up for the trash. Putting on his jacket, he reached for his cup. "Ready when you are," he said.

Annie smiled as they walked out of the warm coffee shop and into the frigid winter air. She worked alone most of the time, except when at the nursery with her two employees. It might be fun to have a ride-along.

The morning was beautiful. The snow covering the ground sparkled like diamonds in the sunshine. The streets were clear enough to not worry about slipping and sliding and the air was incredibly clear as the view of the distant Bitterroot peaks attested.

Once they were in the cab of the pickup truck, she picked up a clipboard with a list of businesses and addresses.

"I plan a circle route," she said.

"Meaning?"

"We'll start out on one side of the street go to the end and the come back on the other side. That way you'll get to see all of downtown and I'll fill you in on the places we're stopping."

The first stop was the welcome center at the edge of town. Annie quickly took in two pots of the flame red flowers, stopping only a few minutes to chat with Marcia, the only full-time employee for the welcome center.

The next stop was the police station on the first side street heading toward the heart of Lamberton.

"Cops like flowers?" Nick asked as she pulled into a parking place right in front.

"Easy Christmas decorations, less bother for them. I also have a tree for them to be delivered later this week–already decorated. They like the festivities, but not decorating so much. More business for me," she said getting out of the truck.

By late morning Nick knew quite a bit about downtown Lamberton. Not that it comprised the entire town; there were several side streets that held offices and a strip mall. A big feed and seed store on another one side street, and several small businesses on each of the cross streets. But for Main Street, Annie had a story about each business as they passed or stopped.

"That's the last of them," she said when she returned from a delivery almost opposite the first stop.

"Do you volunteer at the visitor's center?" he asked.

She shook her head. "Why?"

"You'd make a great tour guide. I feel I know a lot more about the town than before."

She smiled. "Well, I have lived here all my life," she said.

"Don't you ever want to go someplace else? Try somewhere else?"

She shook her head—thinking of Jack.

"I had the chance, once, but couldn't even think of living somewhere else. This is home."

He nodded. "That's one thing I don't have—home, unless you count the suitcase I live out of," he said whimsically.

"Doesn't sound like much of a home if you don't mind me saying," she replied. "Don't you ever think about putting down roots? Making lifelong friends, becoming part of a community?"

"Not until recently," he said slowly.

"Want lunch? The café on Beale Street has great burgers and fries," Annie said.

He nodded. It would give him a chance to find out more about Annie herself. She was a wealth of knowledge about the town, but had told him very little about herself. He wanted to know all he could about the woman. She was unlike anyone he'd ever met.

And he wanted to know what made her so content with living in the same place all her life.

The café was half full when they entered. Like the coffee shop, it felt stifling warm after the cold winter air. After helping Annie take off her jacket, he shrugged off his own. They sat at a booth near the back.

"We beat the lunch crowd," Annie said looking around.

Nick reached for the menus tucked into a stand near the wall. He handed her one.

"Thanks, but I don't need it. I eat here a lot if I don't feel like cooking for one. I'm getting the blue cheese burger, spicy fries and a chocolate milkshake. They have the best milkshakes anywhere."

He opened the menu and looked at the various offerings. While he had eaten in some of the finest restaurants in Europe when on vacations, nothing sounded as enticing as a good old American hamburger and fries. And ice cream was a rare commodity where he normally worked.

"Sounds good," he said. "Only I'll have the mushroom burger."

He closed the menu just as the waitress came to the booth.

"Hey, Annie," the young woman said.

"Hey Jessie. Have you met Nick Keller? He's staying at his cousin Roger's place."

"Hello. Glad to meet you. Where's Roger these days, I haven't seen him in a while."

"He's traveling for Christmas," Nick said.

"So what can I get you folks?" Jessie asked.

Once their orders were given, Nick looked at Annie.

"I know you run a successful landscape business and offer services to suit the season, but tell me more about yourself. You grew up here. Do your parents still live in Lamberton?"

Nodding, she said, "My dad's a manager for the Excalibur Ranch, a big conglomerated-owned ranch west of town. He's been there since I was a kid. He and my mother love ranch life. It's okay, but I'm not a huge fan of cattle. So I picked a different way to make a living. I see them often. It's only a twenty-five minute drive out to the ranch."

"Nice to be close, but not too close."

"Exactly! How about your parents?"

"My mom died when I was in med school. Shortly after that my father married a woman with three little kids. They live in Oregon. I don't see them much. I guess the kids are pretty grown now."

"Don't you like her? Is that why you're here instead of with them?" she asked.

"I don't dislike her. It's just that family is so far removed from mine growing up, I always feel like a third wheel. Plus with kids and all their activities, I thought it better to opt for a quieter place."

Annie felt sad that he didn't feel at home in his father's house any more. She couldn't imagine not being able to go home to see her parents whenever she wanted.

Jessie brought their order, setting them down in front of each of them.

"Are you going to the wrap party tomorrow?" she asked Annie.

"Yep," Annie replied, reaching for the catsup to pour on the edge of the plate by the fries.

Jessie looked at Nick. "If you're not busy, join us. We're wrapping presents from the Santa's Donation."

He looked at Annie in question.

"Santa Donations are gifts people donate for those families on hard times. The first year we held a wrap party on Christmas Eve, but even with more than twenty people wrapping, it took hours when we all wanted to be home. So now we have a wrap party each week to keep up with the donations. It's fun. Join us and you'll meet some more people," she said.

"Are you thinking of settling in Lamberton?" Jessie asked.

"He's a doctor with Doctors Without Borders, just visiting," Annie said.

"Well, come anyway. It's fun and for a good cause," Jessie said. With a smile, she turned to head for another table.

"Where do people donate?" Nick asked.

"At the bins in front of the Community Center. Sometimes it's clothing, sometimes canned goods, and often toys for kids. We have a list of families who sign up for it or others who are recommended, so we know approximate sizes of kids and age for toy match. If a family has a special request, we try to fill it if we get the right donation, or sometimes we buy the specific item ourselves so no one's disappointed."

"Sounds like a terrific way to celebrate the holidays."

He took a big bite of the burger. It had been a while since he'd had a hamburger and, like with the cinnamon roll, he savored every morsel.

Annie had been right, he thought, when he took a sip of the chocolate milkshake. It was ambrosia.

"How did you celebrate in Africa?" Annie asked, delving into her own lunch.

"Sometimes working with an epidemic. Other holidays, I had some days free and visited different cities in Europe. I think my favorite was Christmas in Vienna. What I really missed most, however, was Thanksgiving. Few countries have such a holiday, and none feature turkeys as the main meal. I missed that the most."

"It's a favorite holiday of mine," Annie said. "Though come to think of it, I think most of the major holidays are favorites. You should be here in the spring when we celebrate Gold Rush days."

"I always think of California when I hear gold rush," Nick said.

"I expect more people do, but Montana has a rich history in gold mining. Nothing like the big rush in California, but still, the mines produced millions of dollars worth of gold. Lamberton was a smaller town, but there are mines still scattered around. Most have been cordoned off as unsafe."

"I assume the town was named for a miner?"

"Yes, Josiah Lamberton, owner of the Lamberton Mine, one of the richest. But he was smart and started a store, then a church, then a school, and soon most of lots in the town that sprang up belonged to him. He lived to be an old man, and never revealed the total amount produced by his mine."

"Did he have kids?"

"Six or seven as I remember—all girls. Some stayed, some left when they were married. There're still descendants of his living in town, but with different last names of course."

"I grew up in Portland. We studied Oregon history in school, but I never felt a connection with the founders of the city."

"Small town America, we do things a bit differently," she said with a grin.

3

Nick liked her smile. It seemed to light up her face. He'd worked with female doctors and nurses over the years, even fell for one his first year in Africa.

But none sparked the interest Annie did with her smile.

"Tell me about growing up on a cattle ranch. I assume you ride," Nick said.

"Sure do, and rope and brand calves and whatever else needed doing. I still help out at branding time if my folks need me. And I'd much rather be riding a horse than working the chuck wagon. My mom's been in charge of that for more years than I can remember. One year I helped out and burned some things, served half raw meat, and was banished forever. My good luck," she said, swirling a final french fry in the catsup.

"Planned?" he asked.

"Not really, but if I had thought of it, I would have tried it. No one expects much of my meals.

But I'm a great cake maker. My sour cream pound cake has won ribbons at the county fair."

Nick's mouth began to water even though he was totally full from the lunch. He hadn't had cake in years.

Annie looked at his empty plate and the last of the milkshake. "Are you about ready to go?"

He nodded, draining the milkshake. "You were right, this is great food."

When they reached the truck, Annie offered to drive him home.

Nick accepted, not because he was tired–surprisingly–but he wanted to spend a little more time with Annie.

He told her where the condo complex was. Annie knew it and before long she stopped in front of the unit he was staying in.

"Thanks for letting me ride along," he said, reluctant to get out of the truck, but having no reason to stay.

"Glad for the company."

He nodded and opened the door. Climbing out, he turned and ducked down to see her.

"Do you visit the coffee shop every morning?"

She hesitated a moment then smiled. "Yes, before work if I'm not putting up wreaths."

"Maybe I'll see you there tomorrow. I'm going back for another one of those cinnamon rolls."

They heard a high whimper.

Nick looked around but didn't see anything. Still it sounded like an animal nearby.

Annie switched off the engine.

"Did I hear something?" she asked in the quiet.

The whimper came again.

Nick pinpointed it near some shrubs covered in snow. "There, I think."

Annie climbed out of the truck and walked slowly toward the large bush, Nick joining her. In seconds she knelt and peered into the dim space beneath the bush. A puppy shivered there, whimpering again.

"Oh, honey, what are you doing out in the cold?" Annie said, kneeling closer and reaching in beneath the branches. Snow fell on her from the disturbance, but she caught the puppy and pulled him out, immediately snuggling him against her chest to warm him up. His shivers attested to the cold.

Nick squatted beside her, reaching out to stroke the soft wet fur. Then he stood and looked around. "I don't see anyone looking for this little guy."

"Well we can't leave him out in the cold."

"Come inside the condo. He'll warm up in there," Nick said.

It was a short walk to the end unit condo and

Annie cuddled the puppy trying to get him to stop shivering. Once inside, she glanced around. The condo belonged to Roger Keller, not Nick, so she knew the decorations were reflective of him. What would Nick's place look like? Like a motel room if he just lived out of a suitcase, always on the move.

Sleek and sophisticated were the adjectives that came to mind for this home. Black leather sofa, large TV on the wall, chrome and glass side tables. It was a ubiquitous bachelor pad in Annie's mind.

"Come through to the kitchen. I'll warm some milk and that'll help warm him up internally," Nick said.

The authoritative tone reminded Annie that he was a physician and probably used to giving orders to nurses and patients alike.

A few moments later Annie put the puppy down in front of a shallow bowl of warm milk. The little guy began lapping it up as if he were starving.

"How do we find out who he belongs to?" Nick asked as they watched the puppy.

"We can call animal control. If they don't have a lost dog report, we could take a picture and post fliers around here. He's little, so I don't think he wandered far. I bet someone is frantic with worry."

Nick asked Annie to call while he took a couple of pictures of the puppy and went to his cousin's office to make a flier.

"No one's reported a missing dog," Annie said when she searched for Nick.

"I'm making a flier. We'll print up a few and post them around. Wonder if I should go door to door?"

"Do you know any of the neighbors? Maybe they know who the puppy belongs to," Annie said.

"I've met the Larsons who live next door. And Mrs. Aberthany who lives beyond them. Otherwise I don't know anyone."

"I know Mrs. Abernathy; she is one of the wrappers for the Christmas presents. Let's check with her. She's lived here for years and I bet knows a lot of what goes on with her neighbors."

When they had a dozen fliers, they bundled up, took the puppy and headed for Mrs. Abernathy's.

The older woman invited them in, exclaimed over the puppy, but had no information on where he belonged.

Annie looked at her watch when they left Mrs. Abernathy's place. "I have to get back to the nursery."

She looked down at the puppy. "He's really cute. I know someone is missing him. I used to have a Golden when I was a kid. She was the sweetest dog ever."

She looked at Nick. "Can you watch him? I can't take him with me, I have work to do. And I don't want him to go to animal control until we know his owner isn't looking for him."

Nick looked at the puppy. He knew next to nothing about taking care of a dog. But he was the more likely candidate to do that of the two of them. He had nothing to do this afternoon. Why not?

"Okay, but I'm hoping someone calls after I post the fliers. I put my number on them. So it makes sense I watch him. I bet his owners call before dinner."

"I hope so."

Annie gave the puppy another hug then handed him over to Nick.

"Thanks. I'll check in later to see how he's doing. Call me if the owner claims him, please."

She took a flier and wrote her number across the bottom.

Taking another one, she said she'd post it at her place, but it also gave her Nick's phone number.

Roger's condo had a small enclosed patio area. Nick took the puppy there in case he needed to go. Almost as soon as his paws touched the pavement, the puppy squatted and let go a stream. Then he scampered around the enclosure sniffing the plants and running around. Nick called him and he came right away. Picking up the pup, he entered the condo.

"Here's hoping that will hold you for a while," Nick said, sitting in the recliner and petting the dog.

A moment later the puppy turned around three times on Nick's lap, then collapsed down and closed his eyes. He appeared to instantly fall asleep.

"Good idea," Nick murmured, already feeling himself drift off.

Annie checked in with her employee, Joe, when she reached the nursery. The place had been quiet all morning, but Joe said there'd been several calls about the Christmas trees they stocked. Several people had indicated they'd be by in the afternoon to purchase a tree.

Annie carried a few smaller ones and appreciated the business. The large tree lot at the outskirts of town carried a wider assortment of trees. She felt badly for those that had been cut and not sold or used, and limited her own supply to what she felt would be sold.

"Mac called in sick. He has the flu," Joe said.

"Oh no. I hear that cough lingers for weeks."

Joe shrugged. "Yeah, I heard that too. Hope the rest of us stay well."

Annie nodded and headed for the office. With one of her employees out, she'd have to be available to pick up any slack.

While working on the books, Annie thought about the puppy and wondered if anyone had called Nick about the dog. She'd asked him to call her if the owner showed up and he hadn't called, so probably not.

Joe came into the office. "I decorated the table top tree for the cops. Do you want me to deliver?"

"That's great; we're earlier than the date I quoted. Yes, if you don't mind. I'm about to stop now before my eyes cross. I'll be out front if anyone shows up."

"At least two families are coming after school gets out," he reminded her.

"Right. Say, do you know anyone who just got a puppy–looks like a Golden Retriever pup?"

He shook his head. "Why? Do you want one?"

"No, but I found a puppy this afternoon, over by the Bailor Condos. I didn't see anyone around, no one out looking for their dog. I called animal control but they didn't have a lost dog report."

"Beats me. If I had a puppy I'd take care of it– especially in this weather. We're due for another snow dump before the end of the week."

"I know. At least we know we always have white Christmases."

She needed to make sure she had all her deliveries made in case the snowfall was substantial.

"I'll be back after I deliver the tree," Joe said, turning to carefully pick up the tree and carry it to the truck he drove.

Annie put on her heavy jacket and knit hat. She'd spend time in the tree lot in anticipation of customers stopping by for a tree. The ones near the front were still dusted with snow, giving a perfect example of how a tree might look with minimum decorations but with a dusting of flocking.

She preferred hers with lots of small lights. She had one tree set up on the far right twinkling with colorful lights that blinked on and off.

Sitting on the stool near the cash register, Annie gazed off into the distance, her thoughts now on Nick.

She'd enjoyed spending the morning with him. It had been a long time since Jack Carson had left. She rarely dated, not because she was that picky, but because most of the men who asked her out were ones she'd known all her life and there was simply no spark.

Not that she was thinking about Nick in that way, either. The man was only in Lamberton for a few weeks. Once the holidays were over, he'd be back to Africa.

After Jack, she'd make sure she never got involved with anyone who didn't want to live here.

But until then, could it hurt to offer some western hospitality to a visitor? The thought came unexpected.

A car pulled into the graveled parking lot and all thoughts of Nick fled. Time to get to work.

Nick woke when the puppy began stirring. He picked the little fellow up and immediately put him outside in the enclosed courtyard. Not a moment too soon. Bringing the puppy back inside he wondered what to do next. He couldn't keep feeding him milk. This young pup needed solid food. Only Nick hadn't a clue what to feed him.

He reached for his cell phone, then hesitated. His initial thought was to call Annie and see what she'd recommend. She'd had dogs before, he never had.

He hesitated. He had a medical degree. He'd spent years practicing in some of the most remote areas of the globe. But never the dogs in a village. Just people.

He called the number she'd given him.

"Hi, this is Annie," she answered. "Just a moment, please, I'm with a customer."

It sounded as if she'd laid the phone on a counter. Nick could hear her talking with someone about the cost of a tree. From the way the conversation was going, she sold a Christmas tree to a young family. He smiled when he heard the excited exclamations of the children in the background.

"Thanks for waiting. What can I do for you?" Annie spoke a moment later.

"Share some advice on puppies," Nick said.

"Hi, is he doing okay?" she asked.

"He slept most of the afternoon."

"But no calls about him?"

"Not a single one." He looked at the little puppy running around on the kitchen floor, slipping and sliding if he ran too fast. "Now I expect he's hungry, but I don't have any dog food. What kind should I get?"

"There's puppy food. The grocery store on Ellis has a good selection. Just get a small bag. I'm hoping he'll be back home before long. Otherwise, how are things going?"

"Where is the store exactly?"

"It's on Ellis Street, off the main drag. I tell you what, I'll swing by and pick up a small package of puppy food and bring it by. I'm almost finished here for the day. I can be there in about a half hour."

"Sounds good." Nick watched the puppy slide halfway across the kitchen.

"Do you want to stay for dinner? I could order pizza. That's something I've had several times since I've been here. It's a treat after not having any for years."

"You're on," Annie said.

Nick clicked off and looked at the puppy. "We're having company for dinner. And she's bringing you food, too."

He watched the little dog run around, envying him all that energy.

"I wish I could bottle some of your energy," he told the puppy.

Less than an hour later, Annie rang the door bell. Nick went to answer it and the puppy scampered after him, sliding on the tile entry way as he tried to stop his forward momentum.

It was colder out than before. And the wind had picked up. Annie no longer wore the cap she'd had on earlier, and her hair was swirling in the wind.

"Hi. And hi to you, too, Puppy," Annie said with a big smile. She had a small brown bag in one arm.

"Come in. Don't let him out. I have an enclosed area where I'm putting him in from time to time. So far, no accidents."

"Good. He's a smart little guy. Maybe someone has already started housebreaking."

"I'd think so, but then I would have thought his owner would have gone looking for him by now," Nick said.

She nodded, brushing her hair back from her eyes.

Nick reached out and tucked another wayward strand behind her ear. For a moment he touched her soft skin, still cool from the outdoors.

She caught her breath, gazing up into his eyes. For a moment time stood still.

Then Annie stepped back and handed him the sack. "Dog food."

She took off her jacket and hung it on one of the hooks in the entry way.

"Good, I bet he's starving. Though I did give him some more milk," Nick said, turning abruptly to head for the kitchen. His fingers could still feel the softness of her skin. Good grief was he now becoming delusional?

He set the bag on the kitchen counter and pulled the small sack of puppy food out of it. "How much do I give?"

"I think the directions are on the back," she said, crowding closer, but not touching.

At least he hadn't freaked her out by his touch.

"I don't know how much he weighs though," Annie said, reading the suggested serving sizes.

"I'd say between fifteen and twenty pounds," Nick said, getting down a small bowl and scooping the dry food into it. He set it on the ground and the puppy made a beeline for it.

He made an endearing gulping sound as he ate as if he was in a race. In no time the bowl was empty. He moved to the water dish Nick had placed on the floor some time ago and slurped up water for almost a full minute. Turning, he dribbled water across the floor as he walked over to Annie, his tail wagging.

"You are so adorable," she said, scooping him up and cuddling him close to her. "Should we give him a name?" she asked.

"I don't know. Seems a bit presumptuous. I keep hoping the owner will call."

"Yeah, you're right. Still, it seems silly to just call him puppy."

"He responds to it," Nick said. Do you think that's what his owner calls him?"

"No. I suspect he comes to any name when someone calls him," Annie said. She stooped down and placed him gently on the floor. When he wandered away, she called "Jerome?"

The puppy ran over wiggling all over.

She grinned at Nick. "Care to try?"

He waited until the puppy began exploring again and then called, "Theophilus."

The puppy scampered over.

"I rest my case," Annie said and laughed.

"So much for knowing his name. Ready to order pizza?"

She nodded.

"What kind?" he asked.

"I like them loaded."

"Me, too. Sounds good."

4

When dinner was ordered, Nick and Annie moved into the living room to await the pizza delivery.

Nick's phone rang and he glanced at the caller before standing. "I need to take this," he said, walking out of the room.

Annie could hear the murmur of his voice as he walked down the hall. Soon it was cut off.

She watched the puppy wondering if it was his work calling wanting to know when he was returning.

Nick returned a couple of minutes later. "Sorry about that. It was my boss."

"Checking up on you to see when you'll be returning?"

"Yes. At least checking in. He knows I'm not looking to return until the New Year."

"Are they shorthanded?"

"Not any more than normal. How many doctors practice in Lamberton?" he asked.

"I don't know. A bunch. We have a hospital over near the elementary school. And several specialists. The town may be small, but our population isn't that small. We have a lot of ranches in the area."

She thought a moment. "I don't believe we have anyone specializing in tropical medicine, though."

He smiled when he realized she was teasing him. "Not a high call for such in Montana I expect."

She looked around the austere living room.

"I know this isn't your place, but does your cousin object to pictures or paintings?"

Nick looked at the walls, then back at Annie. "He probably just hasn't gotten around to finish decorating."

"And he's lived here how long?"

"Okay, maybe that's an understatement. He's been in this place for seven or eight years."

"And you, do you object to decorating for Christmas?"

He studied her for a moment. "I haven't decorated for Christmas in years. Usually we are too busy to do anything beyond decorate the clinic we're working out of—if the folks there even believe in Christmas."

"You aren't in Kansas any longer," she murmured.

"I guess I could get a small tree. But then, unless I find any ornaments Roger owns, I'd have to buy ornaments. That begins to start sounding like a project."

"This is your lucky day. We not only have some small trees, we'll decorate with lights and ornaments and deliver. At the end of the holidays, we'll pick it all up if you wish, and reuse the decorations and recycle the tree."

The doorbell rang just then.

Nick rose and went to get the pizza. Annie scooped up the puppy who started after Nick.

"You stay here, no running away again," she said petting him and smiling at him. She could feel his little tail bumping against her. He was certainly the happiest of puppies.

Nick put the pizza box on the small dining table. "I'll get paper plates. What do you want to drink?"

"A soft drink is fine. Can I help?"

"Nope, this is easy."

The pizza was hot and delicious. For a few moments conversation was halted as they dug into the concoction.

When the first pangs of hunger had been satisfied, Annie looked at Nick. "I think this is my favorite meal. I sometimes believe I could eat pizza seven days a week."

"Ever try that?"

She laughed. "No, common sense prevails. But I do like this meal."

"It tastes even better when you haven't had it in years."

"Tomorrow is the first present wrapping party. Do you want to come?" she asked a few minutes later.

"What time?"

"Seven at the community center. We stage all the toys in one of the breakout rooms, away from prying eyes of curious children who try to see what's going on. But the main room is where we set up the tables and wrap."

"I'll be there," Nick said. "I'm interested in seeing how it works. We might be able to do something like that wherever I'm assigned next Christmas."

Annie left soon after they finished eating.

She was already planning to find the perfect tree for Nick. She'd get Joe to deliver it when it was ready.

Christmas was drawing closer every day. For some reason she felt a special need to make it a special holiday for the visiting doctor.

The next morning Annie entered the coffee shop and drew a deep breath. She loved the various fragrances that permeated the air—coffee, steamed milk, cinnamon rolls and other bakery delights. Grateful the line was short, she soon ordered. Looking around, she saw Nick sitting at a table near the far wall. Smiling she headed in his direction. He had a portion of cinnamon roll still on his plate. She knew he'd already consumed some of it from the satisfied look on his face.

He watched her approach.

"Good morning," she said, "Is this seat taken?"

"Not at all. Join me."

"You're a bad influence," she said, shrugging out of her jacket. "I ordered the cinnamon roll to go with my coffee. I believe it has a gazillion calories."

"You'll burn them up in no time as cold as it is outside."

"Let's hope so."

Her order was called and she quickly picked it up and returned to the table.

"Are you going to be home this morning?" she asked as she bit into the delicious roll.

"After about ten. I let the puppy out and fed him, now I'm on my walking routine. I plan to go home after that. Still no calls from anyone to whom the pup might belong."

"Depending on how the morning goes, I can deliver your tree before noon if that works."

"You do know it won't be safe on the floor with that puppy."

"I know. It's a small tree, prefect for the table near the window. I hope he doesn't knock against it and knock it over. But if so, we'll manage."

"Sounds like a plan."

When they finished eating, Annie rose to head for work. Nick escorted her outside and waited until she got into her truck.

Annie watched as he walked down the sidewalk, aglow from spending time with him at the start of her day. She'd make the coffee shop her first stop from now on!

Annie arranged for Joe to deliver the tree once it was decorated. She focused on the paperwork that needed handling. By mid afternoon she was all caught up. She wandered out into the nursery to check on things. If Joe had needed her, she knew he would have let her know. There were a couple of people in the tree lot. And another in the accessories section of the open air nursery. With Mac still out sick, she needed to be more available for customers.

As the day wound down, anticipation began to rise. She couldn't wait to see Nick again. To introduce him around and have him be part of the present wrapping tonight.

Entering the community center shortly before seven, she was instantly greeted by others already inside. She put her jacket on the coat rack on one wall and headed toward the first table.

Glancing around, she didn't see Nick. She hoped he was still coming.

"Hi Annie, good to see you," Marilyn greeted her. She had been a friend of Annie's since they'd been in high school and Marilyn's family moved into town when her father had set up his dentistry practice.

"Hi." She gave her friend a hug. "Looks like we have a lot to wrap tonight," she said, looking at all the toys on the table. Marvelle Pointe was handing out rolls of wrapping paper to those already at the table.

"Hi Marvelle," Annie said when the woman put a roll near her.

"Hi, Annie. You know the drill–plenty of scissors and tape on all the tables. Holler when you need more paper."

Marvelle moved to the next table.

Annie pulled up a stool and selected a toy truck to wrap for some little boy.

"Wow, look what just walked in," Marilyn said staring over by the double doors.

Annie turned to look, recognizing Nick. She waved and he headed in her direction.

"You know him?" Marilyn murmured.

"Yes, and you will too in a minute."

Annie made introductions and pointed out where Nick could hang his jacket. While he was walking away, Marilyn leaned closer. "He's gorgeous. How long is he staying?"

"Just over the holidays."

"Too bad. He's someone I'd love to get to know."

When he returned, Annie explained how the system worked and he picked up a toy to wrap.

"So Annie said you'll be here over the holidays. Visiting family, Nick?" Marilyn said.

He glanced at Annie with a questioning look.

She smiled.

Marilyn looked from one to the other. "So give," she invited.

"Not much to tell. I'm with Doctors Without Borders, on leave for the holidays."

" What made you pick Lamberton?" she persisted.

"Free place to stay. My cousin's Roger Keller and he offered."

"I know Roger. He never told me he had a cousin at Doctors Without Borders."

"And why would he, you hardly know him," Annie said. "It's not as if you two have exchanged family information."

"True. But I see him in church most Sundays."

"And how often do you chat with him?"

"At least once a year," Marilyn said with a wide smile. "Okay, point taken. We're glad you're helping out tonight, Nick."

"It sounded like worth-while project."

"How long have you known Annie?"

"About three days, right?" he asked, turning to look at her.

"Yep." It seemed longer.

If Marilyn was going to continue her inquisition, Annie wished she ask questions Annie didn't have the answers for so she could learn more about the man who was occupying more and more of her thoughts.

Just then there was a commotion at the door when four cowboys came in full of high spirits. People from all over the room called out greetings. Nick turned to watch the men. They shrugged off heavy coats, tossing them on a chair near the door.

In only moments they were picking up presents and heading for open seats along the tables.

One sat next to Annie.

"Hey, sweet thing," he said as he sat down. He leaned over and gave her a kiss on the cheek.

"Hey yourself, Brad. I see you brought your posse," Annie said.

"First we do good, then we have fun."

"This can be fun," Annie said, turning to concentrate on the little truck she was wrapping.

"Brad Henshaw," he introduced himself to Nick.

"Nick Keller."

"New in town?"

"Just visiting for the holidays," Nick said easily. No need to anyone to know more details than that.

"Join us after this. A few of the boys and me are going to Stella's," Brad invited.

Nick raised an eyebrow in question.

"It's a country-western bar with dancing," Annie said, as she placed the preformed bow on the present.

"Nick is with Doctors Without Borders," Marilyn said. "He might not want to associate with rowdy cowboys."

"You here to scope things out?" Brad asked.

Nick shook his head. "No, why?"

"I heard Doc Miller is thinking of retiring in the spring. I thought you might be interested in the job."

Brad proved to be deft at wrapping the gifts while talking and keeping an eye on all the activity in the room.

"I didn't know that," Annie said. "He's not that old, is he?"

"I think he's wanting warmer weather. I heard his daughter is in Arizona and he might move there," Marilyn said. "Sometimes in the winter I wish I had kinfolks in Arizona, I'd go stay a few months."

Annie shrugged. "It's not that bad."

"All this week it's hovered around freezing and this is a warm spell," her friend replied.

"So what's a doctor without borders?" Brad asked.

Nick explained briefly and then spent the next ten minutes answering questions from Brad and Marilyn.

With all the help the presents received thus far

were wrapped and stacked for delivery within forty-five minutes.

As they began returning the extra wrapping paper and bows to the main table, Brad asked Nick again if he'd like to join him at the bar. Nick glanced and Annie and then nodded.

"Sounds like fun. I'm starting to sound like a broken record, but it's been years since I've been in a country-western bar."

He wondered if Annie would be going, too. Not that it mattered either way. He was getting tired of his own company and some time with others would be a welcomed change. And he might learn something about ranching and cattle.

Nick had a good head for names and once Brad introduced the others going to the bar, he didn't have much difficulty in remembering them.

Annie watched the men leave wistfully.

"You could still go with them," Marilyn said coming up to stand beside her.

"No." She turned to her friend. "What's the point? I don't want to lead any of the local cowboys on and there's no thinking of getting involved with a visitor. He'll be gone right after Christmas."

"You could have a fun few weeks until he does leave," her friend suggested. "You can't still be pining for Jack."

"I'm not pining for Jack." Annie was quick to respond.

"Well it looks like it from here. He's been gone what, two years?"

Annie nodded. For a moment she almost held her breath, waiting for the disappointment and heartache to hit.

Nothing.

She glanced at the closed door. When had she stopped loving Jack? Why no reaction now when Marilyn suggested she was still in love with him.

"I cared for Jack. But he had to go and I had to stay."

"I know Lamberton has been home all your life, but that doesn't mean you have to stay here forever. Lots of folks move on."

"Like you?"

Marilyn laughed. "If the right man came along, you're darn straight I'd move on."

"Even though this is home."

Marilyn tilted her head a little as she studied her friend. "This is a place. I have a home here, but I think if I fell in love, really deeply in love, this home would become a place I lived and my real home would be with the man I loved. Whether we stayed in Lamberton or moved to Timbuktu, home would be the two of us together."

Annie pulled on her jacket as she thought about what Marilyn said.

"Then I guess I didn't love Jack enough. When he wanted to head back east, I couldn't envision a life with him back there. Here, yes. But not in Chicago."

"Just don't close yourself off to possibilities," Marilyn said, giving her a hug as they prepared to leave.

Annie felt a little sad as she drove home. She'd thought she loved Jack. They had been a couple from high school. He'd gone to the university while she began her business, but they'd still been close. Or so she thought.

His plans to move to Chicago after college had startled her. Granted he'd mentioned once or twice that he wanted a bigger town than Lamberton, but she'd thought he was just talking. Once he had his degree and settled down with a job in town, he'd be content.

Two years after he started at the Heller Insurance Agency, he'd asked for, and been granted, a transfer.

She could still remember the night he asked her to marry him. It was right after he received the transfer–and a promotion. He knew they'd be great in Chicago.

She'd argued she wasn't thinking of moving out of Lamberton. She has her fledgling business, her family, all their friends.

All he talked about was the new adventure, the excitement of a major metropolitan city.

It sounded horrible to Annie–to be in a large city where neighbors didn't know their neighbors, where she'd have no friends, probably no job prospects.

Pulling in to the parking place at her apartment, she cut the engine. No point in thinking about the past. She would not have liked living in Chicago.

And Jack loved it. His few letters had shown that. Then the letters tapered off. And finally stopped.

She hadn't thought about him in several months. He never came back for the holidays, but insisted his parents visit him. Was he too caught up in city life to remember old friends?

5

Annie stopped by the coffee shop the next morning. She didn't know if she was hoping Nick would be there or worried if he were there, he'd see more into her being there than was warranted.

It wasn't as if she didn't date. Though truth be told, she didn't very often. If she wanted to attend some event and needed a date, she'd accept the first man who asked.

But if not, she didn't.

And she knew nothing could come of spending time with Nick—he'd be returning to Africa before long. And if she couldn't move to Chicago, she certainly would never move to Africa!

While she was standing in the short line, Nick joined her.

"Good morning," he said, nodding to the man behind her. "Do you mind if I join her?" he asked the man.

"Go ahead."

Annie smiled at interchange and then at Nick.

"So you're up early after a night on the town," she said, feeling warm inside that he'd made the effort to get to the coffee shop so early.

"Yeah, well I learned if it isn't the weekend, cowboys don't stay up too late. They get up even earlier than I do."

"Did you have fun?"

He nodded. "Learned a lot, too."

"About?"

"Life as a cowboy. Or if I filter through the bull they were slinging, I think I have a good idea of how they live. But some of the tall tales they told, if true, should be written up in the Believe It or Not."

"Probably most of them were in the not category," Annie said as they stepped closer to the counter.

When their orders had been taken, they sat at one of the empty tables and shrugged out of heavy coats.

"How's the puppy doing?" she asked.

"I think he's getting too comfortable. I put up some more posters around the condos yesterday afternoon, but no one's called. He's been so good, but he needs to be with his owners, not me. I don't want him bonding with me and have to adapt when I leave."

Annie nodded. "Still, it's better than taking him to the animal shelter. He would be in a cage all day."

"Maybe it's your turn to watch him," Nick suggested.

"I'm working. Though I guess I could take him with me." She tried to picture the puppy being content in the truck while she made deliveries or worked on the Santa's Workshop.

She glanced at Nick. "I know, you both can come with me."

"What?"

"Think about it–he can't just sit in the truck if I'm making deliveries or working somewhere. But if you came, when I get out, he'd still have you."

"I thought you delivered the poinsettias yesterday."

"Now I need to finish up on the Santa's Workshop in the park. It will be open for kids on Saturday."

"I thought it was set up," he said.

"The basic structure is, but it needs decorating and I need to get a generator there to power the heater so everyone doesn't freeze to death."

"The North Pole is cold, that just adds realism."

"We don't want to be that realistic. Come on, what else do you have to do today?" Annie wasn't sure why she was pushing so hard, but she'd enjoyed his company the other day. Having him ride along made the time go by faster.

"You're right. We can swing by the condo and pick up Puppy."

"I still think he needs a name."

"No—that seems too much like bonding. He needs to go back to his owners," Nick said.

Annie was beginning to wonder if the puppy had owners. Surely someone should have missed him by now.

Annie checked in at the nursery and picked up a portable generator before driving to the condo to pick up Nick and the puppy. The temperature had barely risen above zero and snow was in the forecast. Glancing at the gray sky, she hoped it held off for the day. It wasn't supposed to be a big storm, so the weekend activities should go along as planned.

Nick climbed out of the truck at the park and let the puppy out to run around. The building looked ready to go to him. There were painted candy canes around the fake windows and gum drops lining the edge of the room. The bright colors stood out in the grayness of the day.

"I have the generator, but need help getting it out of the back. I have a ramp, but it's still heavy," she said, going to the back.

Nick checked that the puppy was still nearby and went to help.

Annie efficiently placed the ramp at the tailgate and then hopped onto the truck. The generator was on wheels with handles on one end to push it like a wheelbarrow. She lined it up with the ramp, then looked at him.

"This is the tricky part. It's really heavy and I'm afraid it'll get away from me."

He climbed onto the truck bed beside her. "How about I take one handle and you hold on to the other one and we see if we can keep it from running away from us."

It was unwieldy, but only took a moment or two for them to get it safely on the ground. They rolled it behind the workshop and Annie fired it up.

"Noisy," Nick said.

"But we'll have Christmas carols playing when Santa is here, so it won't be so noticeable. At least we'll have some heat while we work. I'll thread out the plug and you plug it in to one of these outlets," she said, pointing them out to him.

She unlocked the door and stepped inside.

Going to where the portable heater was, she fed the electrical cord out the small opening in the back wall and felt when Nick took hold and pulled it through. A moment later the heater came on. It felt wonderful in the frigid air.

Nick entered. He looked around. "Kids must love this," he said, noting the mural on one wall depicting reindeer with their heads over stall doors. On the opposite wall was a mural of elves working on toys. The big chair in the center of the back wall obviously held Santa and could hold a couple of kids at his side for family photos.

"Yes, they seem to. We even have people coming from out of town so they kids can talk to Santa. Bill Foster has a couple of reindeer he brings down each weekend to add to the event."

Nick shook his head. "Most years we hardly know Christmas Day from any other day in the field."

"So make the most of your vacation here and enjoy Christmas this year. Maybe it'll give you some ideas for celebrating next year," she said with a smile. "Okay, next up, we need to bring in the Christmas tree in the back of the truck. And get those lights working. I have a wreath for the front door and then we need to set up the counter for registration. We take photos and have to email them to the parents, or make copies here if they don't have a computer."

"I thought everyone had a computer."

"You'd be surprised. There are quite a few families who don't."

They worked harmoniously together. The puppy was curious and sniffed everywhere. When the tree was set up, he immediately began sniffing that as well.

"Watch that he doesn't think that's a tree to pee on," she warned as she looked at the puppy.

"Come on, fellow, let's take you outside again," Nick said, calling the dog.

The puppy pranced over and immediately slipped outside when Nick opened the door.

A few minutes later they returned.

"Duty done," Nick said.

"And we're about finished here. The last minute things will be brought by the Santa team."

"Santa team?" he asked.

"The elves who help Santa bring the camera and portable printer and all each day. We don't leave that here. But the rest is safe enough. We'll turn everything off and be ready to go."

"And the generator is safe out back?"

"Sure. Everyone knows what it's for and wouldn't want to disappoint the children."

When they stepped outside Annie looked at the snow that had begun to fall.

"At least we finished before the snow started."

Nick turned up the collar of his jacket and called for the puppy. "What's next?"

"I need to get to the nursery. I can drop you at your condo."

"Lunch?"

She glanced at her watch. It was early, but she could eat now and have a longer afternoon for work.

"Okay. The café?"

"Best burgers I've had since returning to the States," he said, picking up the puppy and getting into the truck.

Annie wasn't surprised that the café was half empty. With the snow storm increasing in intensity, she knew people wouldn't be coming out if not necessary.

When lunch finished, Annie dropped Nick at his cousin's condo and then headed for the nursery. Several inches of snow already coated the road and she switched to four-wheel drive. Driving cautiously, she had no problem making it to the nursery, but the snow showed no signs of abating so she made the decision to let Joe take off early and close the nursery for the rest of the day.

That left her at loose ends.

She checked everything before heading to the office. It was colder than she liked even with the heater on. Debating whether to do some work or head for home herself, she wished she hadn't dropped Nick off. If he'd come with her here, they might have planned something for the afternoon.

She shook her head. "Don't go thinking of ways to spend time with him. He's leaving after the holidays. And you, my girl, are staying right here," she muttered to herself as she began locking up.

Back on the road she was glad she'd made the decision to close. Visibility was getting worse. Once she had to swerve to avoid a car that had spun out. Stopping for a moment to see if they needed any help, she then continued on her way.

"Safe and sound," she said, pulling into her parking place at the apartment building. The first thing she was going to do was check the weather channel. This light flurry was more like a major snow dump and she wanted to know what more was expected.

Annie had just prepared a cup of hot chocolate to warm up when her cell phone rang.

"Hello?"

"Do you know how much snow is coming down?" Nick's voice asked.

She glanced out the window. "At an estimate, lots."

"And do you know how low to the ground this puppy is?"

She smiled. "I'm sure he's probably belly deep in snow."

"Which makes him not want to go outside to do his business."

"Oh oh, did he have an accident in the house?"

"More like a deliberate. I'm going to have to shovel the patio area to get him outside."

She giggled. "Sorry about that."

"Somehow your tone doesn't sound very sorry."

"Well you did say you wanted cold weather after Africa."

"Next time I'll temper that request. Are you at the nursery?"

"No, I closed up. I doubt anyone is out in this snowstorm for nursery items. And the roads were already treacherous when I drove home."

"So where is home?"

"An apartment complex on North Berryessa Street."

"How far from here?"

"About fifteen blocks, I think. Why, are you thinking of coming over here?"

"If you're home, you can take the puppy for a while."

"Oh, it would be too far for him to walk in deep to him snow," she quickly said.

For a moment she thought about inviting him over. The afternoon stretched out with not much to do. They could watch a movie together. Share some popcorn and more hot chocolate.

But she couldn't ask him to go out in this storm, especially with the puppy.

Or could she? He was a grown man, he could make his own decisions.

"Want to come over to watch a movie?" she said on impulse.

"Only if Pupper can come."

"Pupper?"

Sounds more manly than puppy."

"Manly? He's a little dog."

"Who one day will probably be a big dog if his paws are anything to go by."

"Fine. If you want to venture forth, I'll give you my address and send out Search and Rescue if you don't make it here in an hour."

Nick jotted down the address and directions as he kept an eye on the dog. The little fellow was happily chewing on a toy Nick had bought for him.

"Up for a walk, Pupper?" he asked when he ended the call to Annie.

The puppy wagged his tail, picked up his toy and pranced over to Nick.

"Wish we had a leash and collar. If you walk part way it'll tire you out so you'll sleep a while when we get to Annie's place."

For a moment Nick considered being in Lamberton versus Africa. He hadn't worked in snow for many years, so that was one major difference. And his colleagues often hung out together after work, but he hadn't seen a movie in years, either. Or walked over to a friend's house.

He put on his heavy jacket and scrounged his cousin's clothes looking for a hat. He knew it'd keep warmer wearing a hat. Finally he found a knit cap that would have to do.

"Okay, boy, we're ready."

It was much colder than Nick anticipated. Two blocks away from the condo and he was already questioning the wisdom of walking to Annie's. The puppy was struggling to walk in the deep to him snow, jumping rather than walking, splatting into the snow with each jump. They passed a man already shoveling his driveway.

Nick waved and the man stopped for a moment and nodded, his face lighting in a smile when he saw Pupper.

"Taking the dog for a walk?" he asked as if it were perfectly normal to be traipsing through a snowstorm.

"I'm hoping it'll tire him out so he'll sleep a bit," Nick responded easily.

"Good luck with that."

"Isn't more snow expected," Nick asked nodding to the partially cleared drive.

"Yep, but eight inches at a time is easier for me to shovel than sixteen inches."

That made sense. Maybe he should have shoveled the patio before he left to minimize how much he'd need to shovel when they returned home. Too late now.

"Enjoy your walk."

"Thanks."

By the time he estimated they were halfway there, the puppy began flagging. Nick scooped him up and continued walking.

Annie lived in an apartment building comprised of three floors with several apartments on each floor. He found hers easily enough and knocked, still holding the puppy

When she opened the door, he caught his breath. She looked beautiful.

"You made it. Are you freezing?" she asked as she swung the door wide and gestured for him to enter. "You look like the abominable snowman."

"Take the puppy and I'll brush off the snow here in the hall rather than get your floor wet."

She reached for the puppy and dusted the snow off his head. "Hi Pupper. Glad you came to visit."

She closed the door behind Nick a moment later and put the puppy on the floor.

Taking Nick's jacket, she slung it over one of her wooden chairs to let it dry while he was there.

"I smell popcorn," he said as he took in her apartment. It wasn't large, but looked comfortable and cozy. And it was delightfully warm after his trek through the snow. "I hate to keep harping on the difference, but it's been years since I've had popcorn."

"I made a big batch. I love munching on it when watching movies. I have a subscription , so we can watch almost anything you want. Do you like mysteries? Action flicks?"

"I think the last movie I watched was Lord of the Rings. How long ago was that?"

"A while. There have been a few more made since then."

It took a while for Nick to peruse the offerings and he finally settled on an action-adventure film and they sat together on her sofa, the puppy flopped down in front of them sound asleep.

Engrossed in the movie, they ignored the falling snow outside. The action was non-stop and the good guys won, so both were feeling up beat when the movie ended.

Nick glanced out the window as she cleaned up the popcorn bowl and the mugs they'd used during the film.

"It's almost dark out," he said, rising. "We need to head for home."

She looked out as well. "And it's still snowing. I bet it's topped twelve inches now. Are you sure you can make it back to the condo?"

"Hey, D.B.'s are rugged. We can conquer anything."

She laughed. "Okay, then doctor. Call me when you get home."

"And if I don't make it in an hour, you'll call search and rescue."

"Right."

Annie watched Nick and the puppy as they walked down the hallway and disappeared from view as they descended the stairs. She'd enjoyed the afternoon. Nick wasn't one to sit silent through a film and the comments he made had her laughing. The show was a bit beyond plausible and he caught every extraordinary event.

Wistfully wishing they could spend more time together, she slowly shut her front door.

She hadn't thought about Jack in a long time. But now she realized she missed the quiet times like this afternoon. Sharing them with someone. Making shared memories.

Would Nick think back fondly on this afternoon when he was fighting some disaster or dealing with some horrible disease?

She hoped so.

6

Nick's cell rang when he was still a few blocks from the condo. Carrying the puppy and slogging through the deep snow wasn't as easy as walking over to Annie's had been.

"Keller," he answered.

"Hey Nick, it's Roger. You still at my place?"

"Yes, through New Year's at least. Where are you?"

"In the hospital."

"What? What happened?"

"Slipped on an icy stairway and broke my leg. That puts paid to my plans for soaking in the sun in Barbados for the holidays. The conference ended yesterday, and I fell on my way to a subway station."

"What do you need?"

"Nothing now. But they're releasing me tomorrow and I want to come home. Can you pick me up at the airport? I have my flight booked."

"Of course. Wait a minute, that might be a problem."

"If my coming home interferes with your plans–"

"It's not that. It's snowing like crazy here. It's already almost up to my knees. Will your car handle snow like that?"

Nick had picked up his cousin's car at the airport when he landed. Neither expected Roger to be home before the New Year.

The nearest major airport to Lamberton was Missoula. He knew the major roads would be clear by tomorrow, if the storm stopped by then. But he wasn't sure about getting to the interstate.

"They'll have the roads cleared by morning. Sorry to change plans," Roger said.

"Hey, I'm glad you're okay and it was your leg that broke and not your head."

"Well, I should have my head examined. I was looking at my cell and totally missed the icy stairs."

Nick could hear the disgust in his cousin's voice.

"I'll meet your flight," he said.

He called Annie.

"Glad you made it home safely," she said she answered. "I was starting to get worried."

"It's a lot colder out than I anticipated. And the snow is almost knee deep."

"Better than Africa, though."

"I'm rethinking that. I need your help. My cousin called right as I entered the apartment. Roger fell and broke his leg and is coming home tomorrow so I need to get to the airport to pick him up. Obviously I can't take Pupper all that way. Can you take him?"

"Sure. What time are you leaving?"

"Early, his flight gets in at one and I want enough time to deal with highway conditions, so wanted to leave before eight."

"I can swing by on my way to the nursery and pick him up."

"I don't know how mobile Roger's going to be. It might not be the best idea to have a puppy underfoot in case he trips Roger and he falls again."

"It's okay. He can hang out with me until someone claims him. I'm sorry about your cousin. But that'll give you someone to spend Christmas with," she said brightly.

Nick didn't say anything. She had a point. But he'd thought maybe he'd spend Christmas with her.

"Okay then, I'll see you in the morning."

When he hung up, he went to wipe the puppy off. The snow coating his back had melted in the warmth of the condo and he was dripping as he scurried around.

"I'm going to miss you," Nick said, contemplating the puppy. His lifestyle wasn't conducive to pets of any kind. He'd enjoyed the days with this little fellow.

The next morning at ten to eight Annie knocked on the front door. Nick answered, holding the puppy so he wouldn't dart out.

Pupper wagged his tail when he saw Annie.

"Come in. I put some of his things in a bag and I'll carry that out to your truck, along with the little bed I bought him."

She took the puppy and laughed when he licked her chin. "So up for an adventure today, Pupper?" She wrinkled her nose and looked at Nick. "He needs a better name."

"He's not ours. Someone must be missing him. I predict he'll be home for Christmas."

"Still, how about Buster?"

"Or Rodney?"

"Rodney? For a dog? No, I like Buster."

"Beau?"

"Sounds too much like no, he'd get confused. How about Lucky. He's lucky we found him."

"Okay, for as long as we have him we can call him Lucky," Nick said. "It does sound better than Pupper."

"You all set to pick up your cousin?"

"As I'll ever be. I don't know how mobile he'll be. Enough to fly, so I hope he's not confined to a wheelchair."

"Okay, we'll be off. I don't want to hold you up," Annie said, turning for the door, Lucky firmly held.

In less than five minutes she was driving toward the nursery. "I hope you'll be good today. It won't be the same as with Nick, but you'll be able to run around some and have me for company when I'm in the office."

She wasn't sure how easy it was going to be to take care of the dog. She didn't have a convenient patio for Lucky to use. She'd have to take him out on the leash and wait while he did his business. Still, Nick said he was sleeping through the night without a bathroom call, so she hoped it held at her place as well.

Marilyn called her mid morning.

"Are you available to be an elf for the Santa's Workshop," she asked abruptly.

"What happened to Steph?"

"Came down with a horrible cold. And we don't want to share that with the kids who will be attending. You're about her size, so the costume would fit. I tried Alice and she can't do it, so you're my best hope."

"Saturday is usually a busy day here and the last Saturday before Christmas will spike tree sales."

"Your employees can handle that. Santa's Workshop needs you. It's only for a few hours. And there's no one else."

"Great, okay, I'll do it. But that heater better be working at full blast. Two years ago when I did it, I almost froze."

"Wear long underwear beneath the tights and you'll be fine."

"And look like the Pillsbury dough man," Annie said with a laugh. "I'll think of something, what time do I need to be there?"

"The doors open at ten and you'll need to stay until three. I'll bring lunch around twelve thirty and you can eat when there's a lull," her friend said.

"As I remember, there is no lull. But I'll grab a bite when I can."

Lucky jumped up from where he'd been gnawing on a bone and proudly carried it in his mouth.

"Oh, I forgot. I have a dog," Annie said.

"What? When did you get a dog?"

"Actually it's the puppy Nick and I found in the snow. He was taking care of him but his cousin is coming home and he didn't want a puppy under foot. Anyway, I don't know if he can watch him tomorrow or not. Otherwise, I'll have to bring him with me."

"That'll make the kids' day. So you and Nick own a puppy together? Very interesting," Marilyn said.

"We don't own it, it's lost and we're watching him until his owners claim him."

"So you're seeing Nick a lot, it seems."

"Ummm. I know where you're going with this. We're just friends. He's only here a few more weeks and then will be returning to Africa or somewhere. I'm being friendly. He doesn't know anyone here."

"Well, he met Brad and the other boys from the ranch and me. And he could expand his circle of acquaintances if he wanted. Open yourself up to possibilities, girl."

"He's just a visitor."

"If you say so. See you tomorrow at a bit before ten. I'll see if Clarence will start the heater around nine so the hut is warm by the time Santa opens."

Annie sat for a long time after ending the call with her friend.

She liked being with Nick. They both knew it was just for the holidays. He'd be leaving in January. She looked forward to spending time with him. She found him fascinating. And funny. And interesting. And–

She shook her head. They were friends, nothing more. After he left, she'd still be in Lamberton, still have her nursery and have memories of a Christmas season that was turning out to be a little different.

She couldn't help remembering how much fun yesterday had been. Not doing much–but doing it together. Would she ever find the right man to fall in love with, get married and share their lives?

Jack had chosen another life style. Nick made his home on a different continent. Wasn't there someone for her?

Annie went home for lunch. She started a hearty beef stew cooking in the slow cooker so it'd be ready when dinner time came. Playing with the puppy to tire him out, she enjoyed the break before heading back to work.

Several families stopped by the nursery that afternoon to pick up a Christmas tree. Between customers, she decorated a small table-top tree with lights and a few ornaments.

"That looks nice. Who ordered it?" Joe asked mid afternoon as he stopped by the counter she had the tree on.

"Nick Keller," she said. "I'll take it by on my way home."

It would be a nice gesture and give her a chance to see him again today. The brief handing off of the puppy that morning could scarcely be counted as seeing him.

Shortly before closing time Annie's cell phone rang. It was Nick.

"I wanted to let you know we made it back safe and sound," he said.

"How's your cousin?"

"Cranky."

She could hear his protest in the background and smiled. Sounded like family.

"And is he mobile?"

"He needs a walking cast put on in a few days, so for now it's crutches, but at least not a wheel chair. How's Lucky?"

"Doing well, though I think he believes all the Christmas trees are gathered just for him."

"Oh no, is he peeing on them?"

"Not quite, but he does love sniffing around them and plopping down among them. It's too cold to leave him outside, but he does love them."

"Who's Lucky?" Annie heard in the background.

"I'll explain later."

"Since your cousin is there and you'll both be spending Christmas in the condo, I did up a tree for you. I can bring it by after work," Annie said. "In fact, if you don't' have other plans, I made a beef stew we could all share for dinner."

"You don't have to do that," Nick said. "But I'm glad you did. Sounds good. When will you be here?"

"Around six okay?"

"Perfect. Maybe Roger will want to take a nap by then."

She laughed. "I'm looking forward to meeting your cousin. He can't nap that late, he wouldn't sleep through the night."

"Yes, but if he were sleeping, it'd just be you, me and Lucky. Like it's been."

She nodded even though he couldn't see her. For a moment she felt a flare of happiness. He liked it with the three of them, too.

"Tomorrow I might need you to watch Lucky, though you can do it at my place if you think he's a danger to your cousin. I've been tapped to be an elf at Santa's Workshop."

"An elf? What does that entail?"

"I'll explain it at dinner. See you at six."

Annie couldn't wait for dinner time. She closed the nursery promptly at five. Wedging the tree in the back of the truck so it wouldn't fall, she scooped up the puppy and headed for home.

The delicious aroma of beef stew met her when she entered her apartment. Her mouth was already watering. It was her mother's recipe and everyone loved it.

Feeding the puppy first, she gathered some toys to occupy him at Nick's.

When he was finished, she took the crusty loaf of bread that went so well with the stew, her crock pot and the bag of toys and headed for the truck. Lucky trotted along right beside her.

The roads had been cleared and were no long treacherous as the previous night. Still she drove carefully, not wanting the stew to spill or the puppy to fall off the seat.

Annie parked the car near Nick's condo. Trying to balance the stew and the puppy wasn't easy, but she managed to get to the door without a mishap. Knocking briefly, she hoped they heard her because she didn't have enough hands to knock more than once. The puppy was already pulling on his leash trying to sniff the bush by the small porch.

Nick opened the door.

"Hi," she said with a smile. "I'm here with food and a wild puppy."

He took the leash and called the puppy over. When Lucky saw who now held the leash, his tail wagged at a furious pace as he rushed over and jumped up on Nick's leg, almost topping over with excitement.

Nick scooped up the dog and opened the door wider so Annie could enter.

She headed for the kitchen, stopping when she spotted the other man.

"You're Roger Keller, I'm guessing," she said. "Sorry about your accident."

"Carelessness on my part. You're Annie, right?"

"Yep. I brought dinner."

"That's a life saver. I didn't want to have to eat Nick's cooking."

"Hey, I'm a great cook," Nick protested following Annie into the living room, the puppy still squirming in excitement and trying to lick Nick's face.

"And who's that?" Roger asked.

"Lucky," Nick responded.

Roger looked at Annie. "Nice dog."

"He's not mine, but he is a sweetie."

She continued to the kitchen and plugged in the slow cooker. The stew hadn't cooled a lot, but enough that a quick warm up would be best.

"I have your tree in the truck and the rest of the dinner," she said to Nick. "I'll dash out and get it all."

"I'll come with you," Nick said, dumping Lucky on his cousin's lap.

"Hey, what am I supposed to do with a puppy?" Roger asked, caught unaware.

"Mostly hold him until we get the truck unloaded," Nick said, picking up his jacket from the hook near the door and following Annie outside.

She had the back of the truck open and was pulling out a table-top Christmas tree–fully decorated.

"The bread and stuff is in the cab," she said when Nick reached her.

"I'll take the tree." he said. "I can't believe you transport it full decorated. Doesn't anything get broken?"

"Rarely, we know how to wedge them so they don't topple over."

She grabbed the bag from the cab and followed him back inside.

As soon as the door was closed behind them, Roger released Lucky and the puppy dashed over to Nick

"He's seems taken with you, Nick," Roger said.

"He's been living here for a few days," Nick said. "We found him in the snow. So far no owners have claimed him."

"So what are you going to do if no one claims

him? Seems to me someone would have missed him by now if they were concerned about him. You sure can't take him to back Africa with you."

Annie continued on to the kitchen. She knew Nick would be returning to Africa at the first of the year, she'd known it all along, why did hearing Roger say it make her feel sad?

Nick put the tree on the counter between the kitchen and living area.

Roger looked at it and then at his cousin. "A Christmas tree?"

"A gift from me," Annie said, coming back into the room and shrugging out of her jacket. "I own the nursery on Boswell Street."

"That's nice of you. I don't usually have a tree. If I knew they could come fully decorated, I might have gotten one each year."

"You're not usually home over Christmas," Nick said, clearing off the round table in front of the window. He put the tree there, found a nearby plug and plugged in the lights. The tree was full of bright colored lights that sparkled and reflected on the polished ornaments.

"Thank you, Annie. This is a beautiful tree," Nick said with a smile.

"Glad you like it. Dinner will be ready in just a few minutes. I want to warm the bread first."

"Can I help?" Nick asked.

Roger looked at him and then at Annie. "I'd volunteer but am a bit immobile at the moment."

"Very little to be done," she said.

Nick followed her into the kitchen and lifted the lid on the stew. The aroma filled the air.

"Whoa this smells delicious."

"I sure hope it is. Do you think Roger wants to eat where he is or at the table."

"At the table," he called. "I'm not that immobile."

Annie smiled. She should have asked him directly.

When she took the bread out of the oven and began to slice it, Nick joined her at the counter.

Leaning close to him, she said softly, "How is Roger doing? It must have been hard to get here from Chicago so soon after the injury."

"I expect him to crash as soon as dinner is over. With the time zone difference and the pain meds he's on, he's cruising on pure adrenalin now. A good night's sleep will do wonders for him."

"Then let's eat so he can get that sleep."

Annie enjoyed dinner with the two cousins. They regaled her with tales from their childhood. She could tell they were close, especially since they'd grown up in the same town in Oregon,

"So Roger, tell me, why didn't you go to your parents' home for the holiday when you were injured?" Annie said.

"I might have except they're visiting our Aunt Caroline in Florida this year. It's a trip they planned for almost a year. I didn't want them to cut it short."

"Do they even know of your accident?" Nick asked.

"No. I'll give them a call on Christmas and bring them up to date. I hope I'll be in a walking cast by then and back to normal in all others ways."

"Like you're ever normal," Nick teased.

"More so than you, cuz. I didn't go off to Africa to escape."

"Escape?" Annie asked, looking back and forth between the two.

"I wasn't running away from something, I always wanted to work for D.B.," Nick defended,

Annie looked at Roger.

He shrugged. "Aunt Suzie died when Nick was in med school. Before he graduated Uncle Ed remarried. Seems to me you were doing what you could to get out of dealing with that."

Annie looked at Nick. "That's why you're here, right? Visiting with your father now isn't the same."

He shook his head. "They sold the house I grew up in so they could buy a house together. I don't blame Laura for not wanting to live in another woman's house. But that house isn't my home."

Annie nodded. She understood not wanting to be a third wheel in a household that wasn't his.

"I'm glad you decided to come here," she said with a bright smile.

Looking at Roger, she asked, "If you're from Oregon too, how did you end up in Montana?"

Nick grinned. "Yes, tell us Roger. We want to hear every detail."

Roger sighed. "Followed a woman I thought was my soul mate. Only to have her ditch me a year after I began my practice here. By then I had started to build my firm so didn't want to start over somewhere else. I like it here. I've been here for almost ten years now."

Annie nodded. "I like it here, too. I had a chance to move but elected to remain in Lamberton. My family's here, friends I've known all my life. It suits me."

Nick was quiet, watching her conversation with Roger. He knew she liked living in Lamberton, everything she said or did proved that. Not for her the wild adventure of Africa.

For a moment he envied his cousin. He'd found a spot to settle down. He had his life just as he wanted it–practicing law in a small town, taking exotic vacations when he wanted.

Nick wondered if he could settle down. His life the last decade had been moving from one hot spot to another. Others in D.B. came and went. Some had been there longer than he had. Others gave it a couple of years and then returned home.

Would things have been different if he had a home to return to?

7

When dinner was finished, Roger excused himself for bed as Nick has predicted. Annie stayed long enough to help with the dishes, then got her coat. Lucky recognized the move and pranced over to the door his tail wagging in anticipation of a visit outside.

"Guess he's going with me," Annie said, zipping up her jacket.

"If you don't mind."

"No, but I can't watch him tomorrow during the day. Can you watch him then?"

"What's up?"

She grimaced. "I'm going to be a Santa's elf at the Santa Workshop. Steph came down with a bad cold and we don't want to share it with all the kids. So I was next up on the rotation."

"An elf," he said.

"Yes, costume and all. I keep the kids in line and entertained as much as I can while they wait their turn to see Santa."

"Costume," Nick repeated with a smile. "This I've got to see."

"No comments or we'll corral you into a part."

"I'm too big to be an elf," he said, pulling on his jacket.

"We have other parts—photographer, reindeer handler."

"Reindeer handler?"

"Yes, we'll have reindeer there tomorrow—got to have them around if Santa's there. I told you, one of the ranchers has them and lets us borrow them in December."

"I'll stick to puppy handler. What time do you have to be at Santa's Workshop?"

"A bit before ten. We open at ten."

"I'll be there."

"At the workshop?"

"You don't think I want to miss you as an elf, do you?"

She sighed. "Come on Lucky, let's get home."

Nick escorted them to the truck. He opened the driver's door for her and she put the puppy on the seat. Before she could climb in, however, he stopped her.

"Thanks for bringing dinner and for the tree."

Nick leaned in and brushed her lips with his. He pulled back a bit and looked at her as if judging her reaction.

Annie was stunned and unable to move. She hadn't expected–

When she didn't protest, he leaned in again and kissed her, pulling her into his arms. The kiss when on for several seconds until the puppy pushed his face against theirs, trying to get between them.

"Oh, Lucky." Annie burst out laughing as the puppy licked her cheek. "Yuck."

"Your timing sucks, dog," Nick grumbled.

She laughed again and kissed his chin. "Good night," she said and climbed into the truck.

She refused to think about that kiss until she reached home. If she gave into daydreams of what might be, she could run right off the road.

"So, Lucky, what did you think of Roger? He seems nice, doesn't he. And dinner was fun. And I learned more about Nick. I bet he really misses his father. I wonder if they should get together–just the two of them. Not that his dad should put Nick above his new wife, but neither should he push him away just because Nick isn't as happy with his dad's new wife as he is."

Lucky curled up on the seat and wagged his tail, but made no response.

They reached home without any difficulty and Annie let the puppy do his business before taking him inside.

It was only when she was in bed that she let herself think about the kiss. It had been magical. For a short time she'd believed in miracles. Nick would fall in love with her and stay in Lamberton. They'd become a couple and even talk marriage.

But before she could finish that image, reality took hold. She was growing more and more interested in him, but the future didn't hold a miracle. He was returning to Africa and her home was here.

Still, she fell asleep with a smile on her lips. Nick had kissed her.

The next morning Annie was up early. While playing elf wasn't on her top ten list of things to do, she was glad to do her part to make Christmas special for children. She pulled on long underwear and then the red and white tights for her costume. Whoever said elves had to wear skimpy clothes? She put on the dress, noting it stopped mid thigh. At least with the long underwear she had a chance of staying warm. The hat helped. And the workshop was going to be heated. At least she hoped someone remembered to start the heater early.

When it was time to leave, she donned her heavy jacket over the costume and called for Lucky. She wished she was the one spending the day with Nick instead of the puppy. Or with the puppy. She didn't care much. In fact, if it weren't for Lucky, she and Nick might not have spent so much time together.

She frowned. Was he only spending time with her because of the dog?

She thought he enjoyed their time together. What if he were only being polite?

She fretted about the situation all the way to the park. She made sure Lucky had his leash securely fastened when they got out. He pranced around her as they walked to the workshop. It was cold, and no matter what the tights weren't that warm.

Entering Santa's Workshop a couple of minutes later, she was delighted to feel how warm it was. Santa was already there, moving some things around. Marilyn was at the cash register checking it out to make sure it was functioning.

"Good morning," Annie greeted them. She grimaced when she saw Marilyn in a heavy sweater and woolen pants. "Why didn't you have to dress up like an elf?" she asked.

"I'm behind this counter and am really only dealing with the parents. You're the one escorting the kids to Santa. You need to be in character."

"Yeah, until some child who knows me comes in."

"Not to worry, no one wants to take a chance of getting on the wrong side with Santa. If someone knows you, they'll still pretend."

"Maybe."

"Are you sure this is the best place for a dog?" Brad asked. The extra padding and white beard completely disguised the cowboy.

"Nick's coming before ten to take him. I couldn't leave Lucky at home for so long, who knows what he'd be up to."

Marilyn smiled slyly. "So Nick's coming here?"

Annie looked at her suspiciously. "Yes. So?"

"Nothing. I haven't seen him since the present wrapping."

Annie wanted to defend herself, but though better of it. Marilyn would only tease her if she had a clue that Annie was starting to fall for the doctor.

She looked away as the realization hit. She was falling for Nick. She could hardly wait for him to show up this morning just to see him. She thought about him when they apart and loved being with him. She wanted to learn everything she could about him, and share meals, and adventures, and quiet evenings at home with him.

"You okay?" Brad asked, settling in the large throne built especially to hold several kids with Santa for those families who wanted a photo of everyone with Santa.

"I'm fine," Annie said. "I'll step out to see if Nick's here."

"Have him come in to say hi," Marilyn called as Annie left the workshop.

Annie didn't respond, but looked at the parking lot. Nick was walking toward her. Lucky began wagging his tail and pulling on the leash. Annie released it and the little dog almost flew across the snowy ground toward Nick. No question, that puppy loved Nick.

"I know how he feels," she murmured.

Distracted by others now walking across the snow, she checked her watch. It was almost ten. When the first family arrived at the door, she greeted them.

"You got here early. We'll open in five minutes, but you'll be the first to see Santa."

The kids cheered and the mother nodded with a smile. "I was hoping we would, so we didn't have to stand in line for long. Last year seemed endless with the kids so pumped up to see Santa, waiting wasn't happy."

Another family arrived, the kids running across the snow.

Nick came up.

"Good morning," Annie said with a bright smile. Her heart pounded. Her eyes wanted to take in every aspect of him.

"And to you."

To her astonishment, he leaned over and kissed her cheek.

She stared at him.

"A puppy!" The kids in line gathered around the puppy.

Lucky was in his element, licking every face he could reach and wagging his tail in excitement.

"That's a nice touch," one of the mothers said. "Keeps them from complaining about waiting in line."

Nick's eyes met Annie's. "Shall I stay for a little while?"

"If you can."

She glanced toward the parking lot. More and more families were arriving.

"Unless it gets too cold for you or Lucky."

"We'll manage. Do you get a break for lunch?"

"No, we work straight through to three, but I grab a snack as we go. Marilyn brought lots of popcorn, quick to grab a handful and easy to eat."

"I want to pet the puppy," one of the little girls said.

"What's his name?" another child asked.

Nick nodded to Annie and then turned to the children. He patiently answered all the questions the children had, and mentioned to the parents the dog was a stray in hope someone might know to whom he belonged.

Annie entered the workshop.

"Ready?" She shrugged out of her jacket and opened the door.

The time went fast. From time to time Annie glanced outside–to see how long the line was, not to see if Nick was still there. Each time, she saw he was surrounded by children. As the morning waned, Lucky must have gotten tired because when she next looked, Nick was holding him so the kids could pet him.

"Nice touch," Brad said in the two minutes between kids.

"What?" Annie asked.

"Bringing a puppy. No disgruntled kids this year. We should make that part of the event every year. Maybe have a raffle to give him to the winner."

"Something to think about," Marilyn said.

Annie nodded. It wouldn't be the same

without Nick, though. She was already missing him and he wasn't due to leave for a few weeks.

By the time the last child had given Santa a list of desired presents, had her picture taken and left clutching the photograph, Annie was exhausted.

"I think my face is going to crack if I have to smile another minute," she said, rubbing both cheeks.

"I can't feel my legs. Who knew kids could weigh so much," Brad said, standing and stretching.

"They don't, unless you have four at one time," Marilyn said, counting the money from the cash register. The income from the event went to the local schools.

"How did we do today?" Annie asked, walking over to her friend and pulling on her jacket. Brad was turning off the heater and straightening some of the wrapped boxes that were under the large Christmas tree.

"Better than last year, I think. I have to tally the charges next."

"I'm heading for the ranch," Brad said. "Thank you both for today."

"You, too, Brad," Annie said.

When he left, she turned to Marilyn. "As soon as you're ready, we'll head out and I'm heading for home and warmer clothes."

"You're so cute as an elf," her friend said. "I bet Nick liked it."

Annie shrugged. "If he did, he didn't mention it."

"When did he leave?"

"I'm not sure, after twelve. I'm glad the kids in the afternoon didn't know what they missed. They might have been more cranky."

"Kids don't like waiting in line. They were fine."

"I guess."

Marilyn put the money in a bank bag and turned off the cash register. "I'm ready. I'll deposit the money in the bank and head for home myself. Even using this stool, my back hurts."

"Don't talk to me about your back hurting. Next year, you try being the elf."

Marilyn laughed as she joined Annie by the door. The two walked out together and Annie made sure the door was locked. "I wouldn't look as cute as you," her friend said.

Annie scanned the parking lot. She didn't expect Nick and Lucky to be there, but couldn't help a small hope. The only vehicles left were hers and Marilyn's.

"Is Nick taking you to the potluck?" Marilyn asked as they reached her car.

"No." Annie gave her friend a hug. "Though I might ask him. His cousin is back and they may have made plans of their own."

"I thought the cousin was going to the Bahamas or something for the holidays."

"He broke his leg in Chicago so decided to cancel that trip and come home."

"Ummm, how does that change the dynamics?" Marilyn asked.

"What are you talking about?" Annie asked.

"Nothing. Tell him we appreciate the puppy patrol this morning. See you soon."

Annie walked over to her truck and got inside. It was cold and she was hungry and tired. She didn't know what she was supposed to do about Lucky, but right now she didn't care. A hot shower and warm clothes were all she wanted at this moment.

Nick was sprawled on the sofa, Lucky sleeping in his lap. Roger looked over. "I'd take another beer but don't want to wake the puppy."

"He'll go back to sleep," Nick said, easing Lucky onto the floor. He rose and gathered the two empty bottles and headed for the kitchen. Glancing at the clock, he knew Annie would be finished by now. They hadn't made any plans for her getting

Lucky. Should he call her or wait until she called him.

Unless she was tired of the puppy and didn't call.

He handed a bottle of cold beer to Roger when he returned to the living room.

Roger muted the television. "So how long do you plan to keep that dog?" he asked.

"Hadn't thought about it. We keep hoping someone will call to claim him."

"If it hasn't happened by now, it won't," Roger said.

"We don't know that."

"I'd say to count on it. Then he'll go to Annie when you leave?"

Nick stared at the television, but didn't really see the football play. He was thinking of Annie. And how he didn't want to leave. He'd been wrestling with that fact for several days now.

He glanced at Roger. "Do you ever want a family?"

His cousin shrugged. "I like my life the way it is. It's different from what I thought I'd have. But I was crazy for Darlene. Her leaving changed everything."

"That was years ago. No other woman on the horizon?"

"None that I want to spend the rest of my life with. Why the question? Your life is worse than mine for a family of any kind. And after the way your dad's handled things, I'd think you would be off involvement."

"I'm not big on introspection," Nick said. "But this illness has given me a lot of time to think. And now I'm wondering if it's too late for me to think about a family."

"It is if you keep traipsing around Africa," Roger said.

"Is living here enough for you?" Nick asked. "It's much smaller than Portland. Doesn't begin to offer the same amenities."

"I like it. And I take off a couple of times a year to visit the big city. I think I was made for small towns and the easy-going lifestyle. What's going on? You sweet on Annie? Seeing yourself staying?"

Nick shook his head. He wasn't going to discuss his feelings for Annie or the vague discontent he was feeling with his career. It was probably only the after effects of his illness. Once he was back in fighting form, he'd be fine.

They watched the rest of the football game in companionable silence. Nick was glad his cousin didn't push. But it didn't change things. He needed to make some decisions–and soon. His leave was up in early January.

When the game ended, he called Annie.

"Hi," she said. "Want me to come get Lucky?"

"No. I can bring him by your place. Want to get dinner together?"

"Sure. Any place in mind?"

"It's your town, I don't know any place beyond the café."

"We have a great barbeque place beyond the feed barn. Want to try that?"

"Sounds good. I'll pick you up in about a half hour?"

"See you then."

He clicked off and met Roger's eyes. "Want me to bring you something from the barbeque place?"

"Not including me in the invitation?" Roger asked, amusement dancing in his eyes.

"Not this time. But I'll leave Lucky with you for company."

"Great. Yea, bring me back an order of baby back ribs."

When Nick knocked on Annie's door, she opened it quickly. Looking at him she smiled, then glanced behind him. "No Lucky?"

"He's with Roger. I didn't think they'd let him in the restaurant."

"No, I don't suppose they would. Come in. I'll get my jacket."

He waited by the door watching her as she put on the jacket and flipped her hair from beneath it. She glanced around and then walked toward him. "I'm ready. I think you'll like this place."

"Roger wants us to bring him home an order."

"Sounds good."

8

For the first time since she'd met Nick, Annie felt self-conscious riding in his car. What could they talk about?

"So how did the rest of Santa's Workshop go?" he asked.

Grateful for the topic, she relaxed a little. "We were busy all the way to the end and even stayed a few minutes beyond the closing time to make sure we gave every child a chance to see Santa. Marilyn said our take exceeded last year's, which is good."

"And Santa's Workshop is opened tomorrow as well?"

"Yes, but later in the day to avoid church time. Don't want to temp folks with kids to miss church to see Santa. And thankfully I'm not the elf tomorrow."

"You make a cute elf."

She laughed. "Right. My life's ambition."

"If not an elf, what is your life's ambition?" he asked, keeping his eyes on the road as he drove.

She thought about it for a moment. "I'm not sure I have a great ambition. I like my life as it is."

"No urge to see the world? Explore new places, see different lifestyles?"

She shook her head. "No. I'm content right here. That's probably hard for you to understand with your background. I take it you are one who likes to explore new places."

Nick was silent for a moment then slowly nodded. "I guess I am."

They reached the barbeque place and after they parked they headed inside. The aroma of cooking meat was all around them. Nick's mouth watered before they even entered.

"Wow, the aroma alone is worth the visit."

She grinned. "Wait until you taste the food. The meat will melt in your mouth, and every taste bud engages for full enjoyment."

While they waited for their order, Annie asked him to tell her about all the countries he'd visited. The majority were in Africa, but he'd got to a couple of disaster areas in the Pacific Ocean. He tailored the stories to sound more exciting than they had been. Mostly it was tragic and horrific and sad. Either disease or disaster, Doctors Without Borders went in to do what they could. It was never enough.

It never would be enough. He glossed over that, but Annie was more astute than he expected.

"You do terrific work, but is it always so intense? Do you ever get to hear what happens to the people you helped?"

"We get follow up reports on the general population. But for individuals, no. I never hear what becomes of them."

"And that suits you?"

He shrugged. "When I was in med school, this seemed the perfect career."

"And now?" she asked.

"It's the career I chose."

She smiled. "No wish to settle down, to make a place for yourself in a community? To have friends for years? Does that sound too boring to you?"

He stared into her eyes and the thought came that it didn't sound boring at all. But he'd made his choice years ago and settling down didn't look to be in the cards for him.

The server delivered their dinners and for a few minutes conversation ceased as they both began eating.

"I was going to invite you to Christmas at my parents place," Annie said when the first pangs of hunger had been satiated.

"You were but now aren't?" he asked.

"Well, you were alone, now Roger's home so I figured you two would celebrate together."

"Actually some friends of his invited us to their place for dinner." He looked at her. "But if I got another offer, I'd be inclined to accept. I don't know his friends. I know you."

Annie felt a thrill of excitement. He had other plans that he'd forego to spend the day with her.

"Then consider yourself invited. We start early with beignets for brunch. We eat the main meal around one and then have dessert later in the evening. I'll drive. It's a ways out of town, so I could pick you up around nine."

"I look forward to it." And to learning more about Annie by seeing her with her folks. And in the house she grew up in. She still had that tie to her childhood. She was one of the lucky ones.

"Different, I expect, from your family traditions," she said.

Nick nodded. "I haven't had Christmas with family in almost fifteen years. It was never the same after my mother died. That first Christmas we felt so lost. By the next Christmas, my dad had remarried and began making new traditions."

Annie felt a wave of sadness. She couldn't

imagine not spending holidays with her family. Didn't he get lonely?

That was one question she wasn't going to ask.

They ordered a to-go meal for Roger when they were almost finished. By the time it was ready, they were ready to leave.

It was snowing lightly when they left.

"I'll take you home and then get Roger his dinner," Nick said as he backed out of the parking slot.

Annie had hoped to spend more time with him tonight, but with the snow, who knew how the roads would be later.

"I enjoyed the dinner, both the food and the company," she said. It was a night she'd cherish in her memories down the road. She was falling more and more in love with the man who would be leaving soon. She should know better. Hadn't Jack's leaving left a big hole in her heart?

But she didn't seem to have any control over this. She could cut all ties now, instead had invited him to share Christmas Day with her. Never seeing him again would be hard enough in January, she was not going to rush the end of their time together.

Ironic, all the men in Lamberton she could fall for and she was a two time loser in the romance department. Why was she attracted to men who wanted more than this small town could offer?

They swung by the apartment to pick up the dog. When they reached the apartment building, Nick walked her to her door making a short detour for Lucky.

"Are you going to the potluck Christmas Eve?" he asked as she retrieved her key from her purse.

"Of course. Did you want to go?" she asked, slightly surprised.

"I want to see everything Lamberton has to offer. Since it's a potluck, I thought I'd bring deviled eggs. It's one thing I know how to make."

"Sounds yummy. It starts at six, but people start arriving by five-thirty to set up the tables. Plus the early birds get the best tables."

"There are best tables?"

"Near the doors. It gets hot when that room is full and being near the door allows us to open it from time to time to cool things down."

"There's more to this than I expected. Can I give you a lift?"

"Sure. Thanks again for tonight." Annie didn't know whether to just enter her apartment and close the door or tilt her face as if inviting a kiss.

She didn't have to make that decision. Nick drew her into her arms and kissed her as if it were the most natural thing. She cherished every single second. Her emotions were spinning. Her imagination ran wild. What would it be like to see him every day? To kiss him whenever she wanted?

"I better get those ribs home to Roger," Nick said when he ended the kiss. But he still held her, as if reluctant to let her go.

"He can reheat them," she murmured, smiling up at him. Her heart raced. Blood pounded in her veins. She loved this amazing man. She didn't want him to leave ever.

And for once Lucky seemed content to sit at their feet and watch them.

"Good night."

She watched him walk down the hall before letting herself into her apartment.

As she was getting ready for bed a short time later, she wondered if she was destined to remain alone for her life.

Or maybe it was time to give thought to leaving.

She sat on the edge of the bed in stunned reaction. Leave Lamberton? She loved it here.

But did she love Nick more?

Where had that come from? She loved Nick. But she hadn't a clue how he felt. Was he just glad to have someone to spend time with while here? Or was he coming to care for her?

Or just waiting until he could return to work?

She sighed. She hadn't loved Jack enough to go to Chicago. What made her even think she could leave Montana and move to Africa? And not just a house in a village, but one disaster area after another.

Did doctors in D.B. have families that traveled with them?

She shook her head, rose and went to brush her teeth. She was crazy in the head to even think about it. Nick had done nothing to show her he'd ever ask her to go with him.

A few kisses didn't mean a life-long commitment.

But her heart didn't know that. It longed for more time with Nick. More involvement. Intimacy.

Once in bed, sleep was hard to come by. Between reliving the kisses they'd shared and fretting over the future, Annie tossed and turned well into the small hours of the morning.

Christmas Eve was a cold day. The snow that had fallen earlier in the week had been cleared from the roads, but clung to everything else. The temperatures never rose above zero and the wind chill made it almost impossible for anyone to remain outside for very long.

Nick had curtailed his walks, staying close to the condo for a quick return. He was starting to feel antsy with the inactivity, but it was so cold outside, there wasn't much to do.

He took Roger to the hospital on the fourth day to get the walking cane. It'd make things a lot easier for them both.

Lamberton had a small hospital. Any major needs were handled by the larger facility in Missoula. But this one had the basics. While Roger was being treated, Nick asked for a tour. Giving his credentials, he was ushered to the director's office. After chatting with the man for a few minutes, Nick was given a behind the scenes tour of the facility. He was impressed with all the equipment and procedures in place. What he wouldn't have given to have something like this for some of the assignments he'd been on.

The people he met, nurses, technicians and physicians, were friendly and obviously liked their jobs. He and his escort ended up back in the waiting room for orthopedics where Roger was waiting.

"Sorry, I asked for a tour," Nick said. "Have you been here long?"

"No, but I still am on crutches because the cast needs to harden before walking on it. Bummer, I thought I'd walk out of here.

"It'll harden soon enough. Come on, I'll buy you lunch."

"Anything to get out of here and not go home right away. Do you mind driving down Main Street so I can see what it looks like this year. Most years I spend in the tropics, but I might as well see what it has to offer in case I decide to stay home another Christmas. Not that I decided to stay home for this one. That was decided for me."

Nick laughed. "Maybe it'll do you good."

"Just drive," Roger grumbled.

After seeing all the decorations and commenting on them, Roger said he was hungry. They went to the café Nick knew. When they entered several customers called greetings to Roger. He returned them, stopping at a table or two to catch up with friends, explaining the cast.

Nick sat at a table and watched his cousin interact with friends. A pang of envy hit him. Roger had it all. Friends, a job he loved, a community to share his life with.

What did he have? Another assignment pending, colleagues whom he'd know for a short time and then they'd go their separate ways. Sometime reconnecting in another locale, sometimes never seeing them again.

It has been exciting when he started. Heck, even five years ago.

But now?

For a moment he looked into the future. How many more years could he give constantly traveling. Constantly putting his life at risk with disease and catastrophe?

"Hey, did you zone out?" Roger sat down opposite him.

"What?"

"I said Phil and I are going to go back to his place after lunch. That okay with you? Do you want to hang out with us?" Roger asked.

"No. I think I'll check out something."

"Okay. Let's order. By the time we finish lunch the cast should be solid and I can walk out of here without crutches."

"You know when you do start walking on it, your leg is going to hurt even more as it heals," Nick said.

Roger nodded. "So I was told. I want the Reuben, what are you going to get?"

The cousins soon had their orders. Phil joined them before they finished. He'd finished his lunch already and was waiting for Roger.

Introductions were made and Phil asked Nick about his work. Nick explained briefly, which satisfied the other man.

The afternoon stretched out before him when

Roger and Phil took off. Giving in to impulse, Nick drove to Annie's nursery.

It was bitterly cold when he climbed out of the car. Walking into the nursery, he looked around but didn't see anyone. Going back to the office, he knocked and then entered. Lucky immediately jumped up and ran over to him, tail wagging furiously.

"Hi," Annie said, smiling up at him from behind her desk. "I didn't know you were coming over. Did you need something?"

"Just a puppy fix, I think. I miss the little guy. He doing okay at your place?"

"It's hard these last couple of days because it's so cold outside. I can't just let him out like you can at the condo, so I'm constantly telling him to hurry up. But we're managing."

"Roger got a walking cast. We could try Lucky at his place again."

Annie nodded. "I love having him, but it would be easier not to have that last walk at night before bed."

"Roger's decided to attend the town potluck," Nick said, taking a seat on one of the visitor chairs.

"Then don't come pick me up. I'll meet you two there."

"Okay."

Is he bringing something?" she asked. "I don't picture him cooking. But then, I don't picture you cooking either."

"Why, is that a slur on men in the kitchen?" he asked teasing her.

"Somehow you two seem too busy to work in a kitchen."

"Not lately," Nick murmured. "Anyway, he's not bringing anything, but I'm still bringing the deviled eggs. We'll be there at five thirty as you suggested. Save us seats if you get there first."

"Okay, will do."

"And there's dancing, you said?"

Annie nodded. "One spot of the room is left open after nine. There's a DJ who plays music for those who want to dance. It's fun. And passes the time to midnight. The music stops around eleven thirty and everyone packs up and heads for the church of their choice or for home. My folks aren't coming this year. My dad says he's getting too old to drive in snow at one in the morning. But I'm not, so I'll be attending the midnight service."

"Short night if you get up early the next morning."

"Yes, but I'll tell you a secret. We watch a movie after lunch on Christmas day and mostly doze off."

Nick smiled. He was looking forward to meeting her parents, seeing where Annie grew up.

The day of the potluck Annie arrived at the center before five thirty. She placed her casserole on the table of hot foods.

Her friend Marilyn had already laid claim to a table for eight near the front door and Annie went to join her.

"Hi, are all these seats spoken for?" she asked.

"Not so far, but I know others will be looking for a place," Marilyn said, placing napkins on the back of the chairs.

"I want three," Annie said, putting her purse on one of the chairs.

"You, Nick and who else?"

"What makes you think Nick is one of them?" Annie asked.

Marilyn laughed. "Honey, I've seen you two together. I can't imagine you wanting to spend the evening with anyone else."

Annie looked toward the door to see if he'd arrived yet.

"You know he's coming," Marilyn said with a grin. "Just be patient."

Annie sighed. "Am I making a fool of myself?"

"No, I think it's cute. And I bet no one else suspects a thing."

"What could they suspect?"

"That you've fallen for the guy. You have, haven't you?"

Annie nodded. She took a breath and looked at her friend. "So much that if he asks me to go with him, I would."

Marilyn was startled. "Wow, I didn't see that coming. You always said Lamberton was your forever home. When Jack—"

"This is different. Nick is different. I can't believe I said it out loud, but I've been thinking about it for days. I'm crazy in love with him and haven't a clue how he might feel."

"You must have some inkling."

"He likes to spend time with me, but is that only because he doesn't know anyone else? He seems content to explore all the different activities we have going on, but is that because it's so different from what he knows in Africa?"

"He seeks you out, right?"

Annie nodded.

"His cousin's home, right?"

Annie nodded again.

"He's a grown man, he could make as many friends as he wants. I know he's spent a couple of nights at the bar with Brad and his cronies. With his cousin home, he has alternatives. I'd say he's as smitten with you as you are with him. He watches you all the time. And I'd say his expression is between total awe and total longing."

"Really?"

For a moment hope flared. Then Annie shrugged. "Maybe. But maybe you're seeing something that's not there."

"Well, I'll study on it," Marilyn said, nodding toward the doors. "He just walked in. And with Roger."

"You know him from church, right?"

"Yeah, but not well."

""Make sure he sits next to you tonight."

Marilyn nodded watching as the two men walked over to the tables that were almost full with food offerings.

It was obvious that Roger was well known and well liked from the people walking over to him. Several pounded him on the back. Laughter seemed to surround them.

"Probably being teased for his leg break," Annie murmured, obviously watching the two as well.

"He's an avid skier and hasn't taken a fall in years. Yet subway stairs got the best of him," she related.

"Hard to live down. Nick's looking for you,"

Marilyn said as they watched him scan the gathering. When he saw Annie he smiled.

"Wow, no wonder you're considering Africa," Marilyn said fanning her face with her hand. "He's hot!"

The two men made their way to the table and the seats Annie saved for them.

"When do we eat?" Roger asked after greeting them.

"One of the pastors offers the blessing and then the committee chair starts releasing tables one at a time. Last year this table was first so I don't think we'll be so fortunate again," Marilyn said.

Two other couples joined them. After introductions were made, Annie stood. "What does everyone want to drink?"

"I'll help," Nick said.

They walked to the beverage bar and asked for all the drinks, mostly water, but two coffees.

They were given the drinks on a small tray with the instructions to bring the tray back so someone else could use it.

The conversation was pleasant as they waited for their table's turn to get in line for the food.

"I don't see a dance floor," Nick said at one point.

"It's filled with tables right now. After dinner, enough people leave that we can remove those tables for a dance floor," Annie said.

"Dancing?" Roger asked.

Marilyn explained the tradition.

Roger looked at Nick. "Are you planning to stay and then attend the midnight services?"

Nick nodded. "But I can run you home first if you want."

"No, I want to see it all. I may have been missing a lot by taking off every Christmas."

9

The evening passed quickly. The food choices were still amazing even as far down the line as they were. Plates were loaded with a wide variety.

As they walked back to their table, Annie commented on the fact there were no deviled eggs.

"I brought three dozen. Obviously far below the number needed," Nick said.

"They probably went first. People really love deviled eggs, and usually don't take the time to make them except for special occasions."

By the time nine o'clock rolled around, families with young children and several older people left and the dance floor was cleared of tables and chairs. The DJ had set up his position and the music started.

"Annie?" Nick asked in invitation.

"Yes." She jumped up and grinned at Marilyn.

"I'd offer, but am a bit handicapped," Roger said to Marilyn.

"No worries. I'm not expecting you to," she said. "I'll sit this out and keep you company."

The first tune was a fast song and most of the people knew the words and sang as they danced. Annie sang with the rest of them, but Nick shook his head. "I don't know this song," he said at one point.

She laughed. "Hasn't made it to Africa yet, huh?"

He shook his head.

Two more dances and Annie was getting a bit out of breath. Then the DJ segued into a slow, dreamy tune and Nick pulled her close as they began swaying to the music.

"This is more like it," he murmured in her ear.

She nodded, totally agreeing. She could stay like this forever. Her heart pounded. Her breathing was still coming fast, but not because of activity now, but because of her closeness to Nick.

They moved around the small dance floor, occasionally bumping into another couple. Neither minded.

It seemed the time flew by until the DJ announced it was the last song. Another slow one. Annie wished the evening wasn't ending so soon. Would she ever have another opportunity to dance with Nick? Maybe he'd make Lamberton his Christmas destination another year.

At the end of the number, he stopped beneath a cross beam and gave her a kiss.

Startled at this public display, Annie looked up at him.

"Mistletoe," he said with a grin, pointing to the sprig hanging from the beam.

She laughed. "And you spotted it. There doesn't look like much."

"Even a teaspoon of mistletoe prompts kisses."

"Hey, move on, give the rest of a chance." A couple stood beside him with big grins on their faces.

Nick stepped back, still holding her hand.

"This has been a special evening, Annie. Thank you."

She nodded. "I'm glad you came."

The church service welcoming the Christ child was moving and traditional. The old carols were sung with love and enthusiasm. The few children attending were sleepy-eyed and quiet. Annie couldn't help remembering when her parents had brought her and how she'd longed to stay up for the midnight service but had hardly been able to keep her eyes open.

Leaving the church when the service ended, Annie smiled at Nick and Roger.

"So we're still on for tomorrow," Nick said.

"Yes. I'll be there at nine. Bring Lucky. My folks will love him. Merry Christmas, Roger."

"Merry Christmas, Annie. And thanks for taking the guy off my hands for the day."

They all laughed and went to their vehicles.

Annie hummed one of the carols as she drove home. She couldn't wait until tomorrow.

Christmas morning dawned clear and cold. Annie packed her gifts in the truck and headed out to pick up Nick. Her mother made the most delicious beignets for Christmas day and Annie couldn't wait to get some.

Nick and Lucky were waiting in the parking lot when she drove up.

"I didn't want you to have to get out," he said when he opened the passenger door.

He put Lucky on the seat and the puppy scampered over to give Annie a big lick.

"Well, Merry Christmas to you, too," she said. Looking at Nick, she smiled warmly. "And a Merry Christmas to you."

"Merry Christmas. He set a small bag on the floor and climbed in.

"Is it too crowded with Lucky on the seat?" he asked, slamming the door closed.

"Nope as long as he behaves. And he has every other time."

As Annie pulled out onto the road, the little puppy collapsed on the seat, his head on Nick's leg. Before they left town Lucky was asleep.

"I wish I could drop off like that," Nick commented.

"You probably did when you were a baby," Annie said. "And we had as much energy as a puppy back then. I think that's wasted on kids. I could use some non-stop energy some days."

"Tell me more about your parents," Nick said.

"My dad's a manager for the ranch they live on. The owner of the property is a conglomerate. Dad's been manager there almost my entire life. He loves the life, but never could afford to buy a place of his own. This is the closest thing and I think it suits him."

"Was he raised on a ranch?"

"No, actually his father was an accountant. Grandpa's retired now. But Dad wanted to be a cowboy since he was about four to hear him tell it. And my mother was raised on a ranch in Texas, so she supports him in every way. Even though I'm a bit biased, I think they are a darling couple."

Nick was quiet for a moment. "I remember my mom and dad together. They always seemed to mesh perfectly. I don't remember ever hearing them fight."

Annie wanted to hear more but knew talking about his past brought sadness so she remained silent.

"I called my dad this morning to wish him a Merry Christmas," Nick said. "I'm going to see him before I head back to work."

"That's good. I hope you two reconnect."

Jason and Penny Tolliver welcomed Nick and Lucky into their home. Before long Nick felt as if he'd known them a long time. They were interesting and funny and the day seemed to fly buy. They even had a gift for him—a warm woolen scarf.

"I can use this," Nick said. "It's colder here than I expected."

He had brought a tray of mixed nuts for the Tollivers. For Annie, he gave a pretty gold necklace with a heart on it. It was the kind that opened and when she opened it she saw a small picture of Lucky.

"So you won't forget him if his owners show up," Nick said.

"I would never forget him," Annie said, fastening the necklace around her neck. "Thank you." She'd never forget Nick, either, but didn't say so in front of her parents.

Her gift for Nick was an all-purpose knife.

Suitable, she thought, for anything he might need in his line of work.

It was after dark when they left. Annie focused on driving on the icy roads. The highway was clear, but she was still cautious in case of black ice.

"It's been a great Christmas," Nick said as the lights of town appeared on the horizon.

Annie smiled. "It has. I'm glad you spent it with me."

Nick reached out to take her hand off the steering wheel and clasp it. "I am, too. I, uh, can't take Lucky home with me. Can he stay with you?"

"Sure. I'll take him with me. He's nice company when I have to drive somewhere. And he loves sniffing around at the nursery. So far he goes in the one area I blocked off for him. I don't want to sell trees or plants already anointed with dog pee."

"He's a great little dog. I do think, however, whoever owned him before isn't going to claim him. It's been a long time now since we found him. We need to decide his future."

She knew Nick couldn't take Lucky with him. And with the lack of any discussion between them, she knew she wouldn't be going with Nick, either.

"I can keep him. He's a sweetheart puppy and

will be a wonderful companion."

And something to constantly remind her of Nick and their joint ownership of the dog for a few weeks.

"He already is. Thanks, Annie."

When they reached Roger's condo complex, Annie stopped the truck but didn't turn off the engine.

"I won't keep you." He hesitated a moment. "I'm going to be tied up for the next few days. I'll call you. Drive home safely," he said, opening the door and slipping out before Lucky could follow him.

"Good night," she called. She watched as Nick headed around the side of the building.

"So it's you and me, baby," she said to Lucky. "Who knows how much longer we'll have Nick."

She wondered how he was going to be tied up in Lamberton, but wouldn't pester him. He said he'd call. She hoped it was soon.

The time between Christmas and New Year's was quiet at the nursery. She'd given her employees the week off. She herself didn't have a lot to do. Accounts were current. Plants were mostly dormant in the cold winter months. The few indoor plants she took care of for businesses in town didn't take long to check on and water.

This was the time she usually spent skiing, but now Annie wanted more to spend time with Nick. Did he ski? He'd said he'd be busy for a few days, but it wouldn't hurt to call and ask. If he couldn't ski right away, maybe later in the week.

Roger answered the phone.

"Nick's not here. Didn't he tell you he was taking off?"

Annie's heart dropped. "Taking off? For where? Portland?"

He had said he wanted to see his father again before he returned to work.

Roger was silent for a long moment. "I think he's heading for Paris."

Paris! Annie felt stunned.

Doctor Without Borders was headquartered in Paris. Was he returning to work earlier than she'd expected? She thought they'd have at least until New Year's Day.

"I didn't know," she said, holding back tears. "I knew he wasn't staying long, but thought through the holidays."

"Yeah, me, too. But he received a call Christmas Eve and last night told me he was heading for Paris.

"Did he take all his things?"

"Well, he only had the one duffle bag, so yeah, that's gone. I would have thought he'd have told you."

Annie could hear the sympathy in Roger's tone.

"Well, no need to. Thanks, Roger. Take care."

She clicked off and sat staring off into space as the tears began to flow. She loved Nick Keller and he didn't even care enough to tell her he was leaving.

10

The days dragged by. Annie was glad she had few customers to put on a cheerful face for. The tears had stopped.

Marilyn had called that first day and rushed over when she heard the tears in Annie's voice. She'd been a good friend, trying her best to find a good reason for the way things had turned out.

The bottom line was Nick had been a visitor and had left. Anything else couldn't be blamed on him.

Annie had seen attraction where there wasn't any.

She felt silly for even voicing her willingness to leave her home to travel to unknown future with a man she hardly know. She and Jack had been a couple for years and she'd not left when he did. How could she feel more strongly for a virtual stranger?

Lucky kept her grounded. She had to see to the little dog when she really wanted to go to bed and pull the covers over her head and stay there a month.

But several times a day and in the evening they went outside.

Annie took him to the vet's and made sure he got all the shots he needed. She also got him microchipped and registered him with her information. She bought a large sack of food and a few tennis balls and began playing ball with him. He loved chasing after the ball and always brought it back to her so she could throw it again.

"You're so smart," she told him after throwing another ball across her living room for him. She couldn't wait until spring when they could go to the park and he'd have lots of room to run chasing after the ball.

She wished Nick could see him. She wished Nick would be there in the spring to play ball.

She flat out wished Nick would walk into her apartment right now!

Marilyn called her on New Year's Eve.

"What are you doing tonight?" she asked.

"Staying in with Lucky."

"There's a dance at the Catholic church. Let's go."

"Sorry, I don't feel like it."

"It'll be fun."

"Maybe another time. But not tonight."

"Sweetie, I know you're feeling sad, but maybe you should try to brighten your spirits."

"You could be right, but not tonight."

"Okay. Call me tomorrow. We can celebrate the new year with Bloody Marys and a movie marathon."

"Sounds like a plan. Have fun tonight."

Annie clicked off her phone and tossed it on the sofa. Lying back against the cushions, she wondered what she could do between now and bed time. Not that she was sleeping that well these past few nights. But a final walk with Lucky and then bed gave some structure to her life.

There was a knock on the door.

Had Marilyn come over to try to convince her to go to the dance? She rose reluctantly. She had to make sure she didn't hurt her friend's feelings. But she didn't feel at all like going out.

She opened the door and stared. It was Nick.

"Hi," he said easily.

"What are you doing here?"

He looked perplexed. "I came to see you. And Lucky."

"I thought you went to Paris. Roger said you went to Paris."

"I did. Can I come in?"

She opened the door wide and gestured for him to come in.

Lucky dashed over to greet Nick. His body quivering with excitement.

"Hey, little fellow," Nick scooped him up. "Whoa, you're gaining weight."

Lucky squirmed in his arms, trying to lick his face.

"You won't always be able to lift him, I think," Annie said.

Her heart pounded. She hadn't expected to ever see him again. And here he was, right in her own apartment!

"So, Paris?" she said.

He put the puppy down and shrugged out of his jacket, laying it across the nearby chair.

He turned and reached out to draw her into his arms and kiss her.

It was a magical as ever. Annie kissed him back, filled with delight to see him. She was curious about where he'd been, but for now she'd take pleasure in having him with her.

He ended the kiss and rested his forehead against hers.

"I went to Paris. Now I'm back."

"Just like that? Paris and back in a week? What did you do in Paris?"

"Turned in my notice, packed up the small place I used as a *pied de terre* and came back."

"Turned in your notice? You quit Doctors Without Borders?"

That was the last thing she expected to hear.

"I did."

"Why? I thought you always wanted to work with them."

"I did. Can we sit down. I'll tell you what changed my mind."

They walked to the sofa and sat, Lucky jumping up beside them. When neither paid him any attention, he turned around three times and collapsed on the cushions and closed his eyes.

"So?" she asked.

He hesitated a moment. "I'm not sure where to start."

She waited, watching him closely.

"Last summer I got sick. I mean really sick. For almost a week they didn't think I'd make it. The convalescence was long."

"The reason you're here, still recovering," she guessed. He'd mentioned it before. "And if you're still recovering, I can see it had to have been major."

"It was. First because after all these years it was the first time I caught what we'd been sent in to help with. For weeks I merely existed while being treated. I was out of it most of the time. Once on the road to recovery, however, I had lots of time to think. When I was awake at least. I slept a lot. Ate whatever was put before me and willed my body to get better."

She nodded. Not that she'd seen much evidence he wasn't in top shape since she'd met him. Except how thin he looked.

"Once I regained some of my strength I had a yearning for home. For the good old U. S. of A. So I called Roger and you know the rest."

"Here you are. I know that part. But not the rest. I thought when I heard you'd gone to Paris that you were ready to take up work again."

"You changed that," he said slowly, reaching out to clasp her hand, threading his fingers through hers.

"Me?" she squeaked. That was totally unexpected.

"You and your hometown."

"I don't get it."

"You might not. You haven't yearned for a place of your own for most of your adult life. You haven't wondered what it would be to set down roots, know neighbors for years instead of only however long an outbreak or disaster lasts. You haven't had to worry about what you might be missing from traditions, close ties, family. You have it all. You're happy here and it radiates from you. I wanted some of that."

"Really?" she asked.

"Really. I'm thirty-eight years old, Annie. If I don't make a change now, then when? I don't want to be too old to be a father. Too old to establish ties somewhere, start traditions that will continue after I'm gone from the earth. I want to have long-time friends, shared memories and a future to look forward to."

Anne watched as he spoke. His dark eyes looked deeply into hers. She felt the tension in him and the conviction of what he was saying.

"And you found it in Lamberton?"

"No, I found my hope in you."

"Me?" Her heart began to beat rapidly, her breathing came in short bursts.

"I know we haven't known each other for long, but for me love hit me like a ton of bricks. I can't see anyone else but you. I can't think of anything else but you. I have nothing to offer—no job, no home, only the assurance that if you take a chance with me, I'll do all in my power to make sure you never regret it. Will you marry me?"

"Marry you?" She felt stupid repeating his words, but she was stunned. Was she dreaming?

"I know it's too soon to ask. We could have a long engagement so you could get to know me better. See what we might build together."

"I was ready to go to Africa with you," she said breathlessly.

"What?"

"I know, crazy, right? But I would have gone in a heartbeat if you'd asked me. Now you want to stay here? In Lamberton?"

"If I can get work. Otherwise we might have to find another place. Not too far since I know you'd want to be near your parents. You'd have gone to Africa?" he said in confusion.

She nodded. "I was devastated when Roger said you'd gone to Paris. I thought you'd left for good and hadn't even said goodbye."

"I left a note for you. Didn't he give it to you?"

She shook her head. "No. I haven't seen him. I called one day."

"Idiot, you'd think a lawyer would know the importance of communications."

"You're here now. And I'm glad."

"Are you? Would you consider sharing your life with me, Annie?"

"Yes, yes, yes." She threw her arms around his neck and kissed him.

Delight bubbled up and spread through every cell of her being. Nick loved her! Maybe even as much as she loved him.

Sometime later, they moved into the kitchen to fix some food.

"It'll be next year soon," Nick said with a glance at the clock. "I'm surprised you're home on your own tonight."

She smiled at him. "Who else would I want to be with? If I couldn't be with you, I was content to be on my own. What if I hadn't been home?"

"I'd have waited. Or come back in the morning." He leaned over and brushed his lips against hers in a quick kiss. "I'm glad you were home, though."

They ate the snack, giving a doggie bone to Lucky when he followed them into the kitchen.

Nick looked at the puppy. "He's ours, I guess. I can't believe no one has contacted me about him. He's a sweet little guy."

"Who will probably grow into a sweet big guy. I think you're right, however. With calls to the vets around here and the county animal control, posters, word of mouth—if his owner was anywhere around he'd know how to get him back.

"So we need a house with a yard for him," Nick said. "Big enough for a swing set in the future." He glanced at her.

She was grinning broadly. "I'm all for that!"

"So I thought about going to see my father next week. Would you come with me?"

She nodded.

"I, uh, I wasn't sure you'd want to get engaged," he said. "So I don't have a ring. Shall we go shopping for one as soon as the stores open?"

She nodded, her heart blossoming in happiness. "I love you, Nick."

"I love you, Annie. And I always will."

He sealed that promise with a kiss.

Did you enjoy this story?
If so you may enjoy
The Cowboy's Special Christmas

If you enjoyed **Teaspoon of Mistletoe,** please
consider leaving a review.

For a complete list of Barbara's books, please visit
www.barbaramcmahon.com.

www.ingramcontent.com/pod-product-compliance
Lightning Source LLC
Chambersburg PA
CBHW072228190626
46809CB00017B/1520